THE TRAVELLER'S HAT

THE
TRAVELLER'S
HAT

Liza Potvin

To Keith,
With thanks for
your reading of an
earlier version!
Liza.

RAINCOAST BOOKS

Vancouver

Raincoast Books acknowledges the ongoing financial support of the
Government of Canada through The Canada Council for the Arts and the
Book Publishing Industry Development Program (BPIDP); and the
Government of British Columbia through the BC Arts Council.

Edited by Elizabeth McLean
Text design by Ingrid Paulson
Typeset by Teresa Bubela

NATIONAL LIBRARY OF CANADA CATALOGUING IN PUBLICATION DATA

Potvin, Elizabeth Ann, 1958-
   The traveller's hat / Liza Potvin. — 1st ed.

   ISBN 1-55192-594-X

   I. Title.
PS8581.O8328T72 2003   C813'.6   C2002-911399-7
PR9199.4.P67T72 2002

LIBRARY OF CONGRESS CONTROL NUMBER: 2002096038

Raincoast Books   *In the United States:*
9050 Shaughnessy Street   Publishers Group West
Vancouver, British Columbia   1700 Fourth Street
Canada V6P 6E5   Berkeley, California
www.raincoast.com   94710

At Raincoast Books we are committed to protecting the environment and
to the responsible use of natural resources. We are acting on this commitment
by working with suppliers and printers to phase out our use of paper
produced from ancient forests. This book is one step toward that goal.
It is printed on 100% ancient-forest-free paper (100% post-consumer
recycled), processed chlorine- and acid-free, and supplied by New Leaf
paper. It is printed with vegetable-based inks. For further information,
visit our website at www.raincoast.com. We are working with Markets
Initiative (www.oldgrowthfree.com) on this project.
Printed in Canada by Friesens

10 9 8 7 6 5 4 3 2 1

To Kazz and Forrest,
my sun and moon.

Contents

Let him that would move the world, first move himself.

— Socrates

[Zeus] bade famous Hephaestus make haste and mix earth with water and to put in it the voice and strength of human kind, and fashion a sweet, lovely maiden-shape, like to the immortal goddesses in face; and Athena to teach her needlework and the weaving of the varied web; and golden Aphrodite to shed grace upon her head and cruel longing and cares that weary the limbs. And he charged Hermes the guide, the Slayer of Argus, to put in her a shameless mind and a deceitful nature ... and the Herald of the gods put speech in her. And he called this woman Pandora, because all who dwelt on Olympus gave each a gift, a plague to men who eat bread.

— Hesiod, Works and Days ll.60–82

Sing, O Muse, of the son of Zeus and Maia, lord of Cyllene and Arcadia rich in flocks, the messenger of the gods and bringer of luck, whom Maia of the beautiful hair bore after uniting in love with Zeus ... she brought forth to the light a child and a remarkable thing was accomplished; for the child whom she bore was devious, winning in his cleverness, a robber, a driver of cattle, a guide of dreams, a spy in the night, a watcher at the door, who soon was about to make manifest renowned deeds among the immortal gods ... He was born at dawn, by midday he was playing the lyre, and in the evening he stole the cattle of far-shooting Apollo.

The old man spoke to him in answer: "My friend, it is hard to tell everything that one sees with one's eyes. For many wayfarers pass along the road; some travel intent on much evil; others on much good."

— Homer, The Homeric Hymn to Hermes (number 4)

Assumptions

open your flesh, people, to opposites
conclude the bold configuration, finish
the counterpoint: sky, include earth now.
Flying, a long vole of descent
renders us land again.
Flight is intolerable contradiction.
We bear the bursting seeds of our return
we will not retreat; never be moved.
Stretch us onward include in us the past
sow in us history, make us remember triumph.
— Muriel Rukeyser, "Theory of Flight"

MY FATHER WAS DESCENDED FROM A PEPSI, OR A rotten-tooth, as the lowlife francophones like my grandfather were called in Belle Rivière. In the twilight hours of humid Ontario evenings, you can still see these shackers sitting on the wide stoops of their decrepit tarpaper houses, drinking ale and flinging the bottles onto the porch. Most sported sweat-grimed undershirts stretched tautly over what they proudly referred to as their "Molson's muscles." In their teens and early twenties, they wore tight trousers and strutted down the streets or drove fast cars; they believed they were big-time operators, smooth and immortal, intact. The lucky ones had jobs in nearby Tecumseh or a half-hour's drive across the bridge in Flint, working in the auto plants and making decent money, which they squandered on enormous RCAs and Chevrolets. Those who were not blessed with good luck spoke to their wives and children through bars. And no Pepsi could gain the respect of the Anglos until he could afford a month in Florida every winter; a Miami tan was worn like a badge in lower Ontario, where the last thing anyone wanted was camouflage.

The youngest boy from a family of twenty-two, my father would feel each sweltering supper hour melt into early evening. As summer took over, he watched the acrid sun sink into the steam of nightfall. It never really cooled down enough to sleep at night for more than a few hours. He sat on the stoop alongside his siblings and garrulous neighbours. He scuffed his sandals against the rotting porch deck and listened to the gossip, turning his head first to face one person on his left side and then to another on his right side. When he realized that this sideways glancing would get him nowhere, my father turned his gaze upward instead. Whether it was from a quickness of mind, impatience, or both, he recognized that flying away was more expedient than running away. My father was noted in school as an ace with numbers who painted model airplanes and had serious thoughts about the sky and the planets. He was only seventeen when he joined the Royal Canadian Air Force. Given full gold wings, he wore the RCAF insignia imprinted on the centre of the crest on his shoulder, where it divided into rich black and red embroidered patterns. He was also given a language of precision, designed to say everything necessary for the rebuilding of postwar empires, a brown leather jacket, and a ready-made self-regard. He cruised at high altitudes in his Lancaster Mark II. Yet none of these things could ever mask my father's lifelong sense of inferiority: a French-Canadian stationed in France, whose accent was never pure enough, whose unerasable *joual* earned him as much teasing in the bistros there as it did in the taverns of English Canada. My father never got to see combat, so he invented his own. And thus we became a part of his personal war.

We were living in the barracks near Metz one grey French winter, and my father was trying to decide where we should go for a brief spring holiday. " 'Bout time I get some goddam R 'n R," he said, slurring his words. My mother wanted to go somewhere warm. But her suggestions for possible holiday destinations were shot down immediately. She put up no struggle. My father's air force buddy Karl had been the one to suggest going for mussels in Brussels. The two of them were sitting at the kitchen table late one night, drinking and smoking, and snatches of their loud conversation drifted up the stairs as I was falling asleep. I was nine years old, but accustomed to my father's drinking binges. Most nights when my father drank in the kitchen, he sank into one of his accusatory moods, and we could hear him yelling at my mother, dark and horrible noises that filled the barracks and spilled over into our dreams. I was the eldest, and he hated me the most for not being a son he could be proud of. When he remembered that my mother had forgotten to give him a boy yet, he would turn to me in gradual recognition of my face and spit in it with the slow calmness of the alcoholic whose gestures become almost graceful through habituation.

But on this night he was excited, full of plans. "*Bébert*, keep your voice *down*," my mother kept interjecting, but to no avail. My father had prepared one of his favourite dishes for supper, rabbit stew. Years later my middle sister Odette revealed, with a shudder in her voice, his cooking secret. He bled the freshly killed hare's blood from its neck directly into the stewing pot. Now I am not so certain I would relish the taste of the stew as much as I used to. Yet certain smells alone can take me back to that evening. The slow-cooking aroma had filled our tiny officer's quarters for days, and that night I had taken great pleasure in ladling the rich stew over my spaghetti, removing the delicate bones after my teeth found them. Karl's boisterous appreciation and numerous bottles of local red wine increased my father's delight. The two of them began talking food, which led to memory, which led to travel and the scheme of driving to Brussels two weeks later to eat mussels. It was not until many years later the phrase "mussels in Brussels" would acquire a wistfulness, become a family anecdote, a litany of better times.

We were all duly packed into the rusty Citroën: three girls cramped into the back, our legs perched on top of the suitcases, our immobility making it easier to pinch one another. "I'm going to give you what you deserve if you don't sit still," my father threatened. "But she's asking for it," my youngest sister Francine responded, and I dug my nail harder into her thigh to make her be quiet. "That's it! I've had enough!" he would explode. "Everybody out now for some fresh air!" We would run before he caught us and vented his anger. Usually this involved his removing his air force belt and bending us across his knee until our bottoms were so sore we could not sit without weeping. But he also made it clear that he would not put up with such weaknesses as tears, so we learned not to whimper after he strapped us. We pretended to be entranced by the wildflowers across the field where we stopped, and flew off to gather a bouquet for our mother. The drive took the better part of the first day, but we made many stops to sniff out bakeries that

sold Easter breads, then ate and slept at a small family
hotel. It was drizzling a bit as we approached Brussels
early the next morning, settled into our *pension*,
unloaded all the bottles my father had consumed in the
car into the trash bin, and got ready to go out.

Mostly I remember that day as the first occasion to
wear my shiny new patent leather shoes. Every spring
my father handed my mother money to buy us girls new
shoes. He was insistent that we should have the best
leather. His own feet were badly deformed and he
suffered from hammertoes, a condition made worse by
his being the last in line for hand-me-down shoes. I have
maintained, although often been unable to afford, a taste
for elegant leather shoes. I was wearing my new Easter
shoes for the first time that April when we climbed up
three sets of stairs to arrive at the restaurant Karl had
recommended to my father. I also had on new white
knee socks that offset the black patent leather in a very
pleasing way, I thought, as I clicked my heels together
in what my dance teacher called *plié*, almost as if my
shoes had wings. I could see my face in my shoes all the
way up the stairs, they shone so much! My father poked
his finger into my backside from the step below me, too
hard, until I winced in pain. "Hurry up! You're as bad as
your mother," he said. Impatiently, he took the stairs
two at a time until he passed in front of me, then turned
back to urge me to move faster once more.

On the very top floor, in a small room, we were seated at a table with a red and white gingham cloth. My mother, who was wearing a green suit she had made herself after seeing a similar ensemble worn by Jackie Kennedy in a fashion magazine, reminded us to remember our manners. "Especially you. And don't wipe your snotty nose on the napkin," my father snarled at me. I could smell the stale wine fumes on his breath from all the way across the table. My mother folded her own cloth napkin neatly in her lap and passed the breadbasket to my father.

And then the mussels began to arrive, plateful after steaming plateful, platters of mussels smothered in tomato sauce, others in garlic and butter, some marinated in wine and herbs. The smell in the air was heavenly, all yeasty warm from the bread, and freshly sautéed garlic teased my nose, but I could tell from my father's stern glance that this was one of his moments of glory, not to be interrupted by my enthusiastic comments under any circumstances. And I knew well enough not to touch the food until he had helped himself first. "Children need to be seen and not heard," my mother's echoing of his admonition, seemed to ring in my ears. Before we were allowed to dig into them, my father made us fold our hands: "*Seigneur, nous vous prions ...*" He had already had too much wine and his face was overly ruddy for this early hour. Yet I had never expected that he would make us say grace or that he might expose our family prayer rituals so publicly. He expected us to feel beholden to him, to remember that these were the very best mussels, that May would bring the smaller Danish mussels, that we were here just in time. I am not sure why I felt so mortified, since it was a Catholic city and the waitress and other patrons never took any notice of us. I believe my father wanted our everlasting gratitude for his bounty when he spread his hands and said, "Let us have grace." I gripped my fingers tightly against the backs of my hands and lowered my head in prayer, but again, all I could smell and breathe and think was garlic.

Suddenly he noticed me beside him, turned his head to look below the table, and said, "What are you wearing those ridiculous stockings for? They make your knees look like fat sausages." I wilted. Suddenly my new shoes seemed tawdry, and my pretension of patent leather glamour, a sham. My stomach churned as it usually did when he made comments about my ugliness. For thirty years thereafter I believed I was ugly, and made it a habit not to look in mirrors. I caught my mother's glance briefly before she turned to watch the waiter moving toward the table with more food. I had learned long ago that my mother always took my father's side, and always did exactly as he said. She was beautiful in that quiet moment, her head downcast, in spite of the marks he had left across her cheek the night before, and I secretly believed that I resembled her just a little. I prayed until I finally found something I could be grateful to God

about: at least we were in a restaurant, and chances were
that I wouldn't get the usual whack across the back
of my head when my father was displeased with me.
In public he was the model father. All I could do was
make the sign of the cross against my forehead, lips and
chest, and ask God why I had to have a father who could
be so mean to all of us in one moment, and so generous
in the next. I was learning that not everything that is
incredible is untrue.

Pewter-coloured buckets filled with French fries
arrived at his elbows, and we set to the meal. Enormous
platters were placed ceremoniously in the centre of the
table and were soon laden with our empty mussel shells,
mountains of blue-black shells with undersides as shiny
as dreams. But I cannot really remember what the
mussels tasted like. I was too distraught and angry with
God for being unfair. I do remember that it was the first
time I didn't have to drink my wine watered down, only
because in his distraction my father forgot. And that,
after a crisp green salad, another accompaniment arrived
at our table: the first white asparagus spears of the spring
season, wrapped in wilted leeks tied into bows, drizzled
with butter, parsley and pepper, and served on a red
platter. It was the prettiest dish on the table. Biting one
of those white asparagus tips, I thought I had never
tasted any vegetable so divine, a texture at once luxu-
rious and simple. In all of my culinary quests since,
there has never been any comparison. If I have any taste

today, if my hunger is inspired and rampant, I attribute
it to that first taste of white asparagus.

LATER THAT AFTERNOON WE TOURED BRUSSELS.
It is a city whose palaces, museums and basilicas have a
rich Gothic texture. But for me the former guildhalls in
the Broodhuis inspired a certain chill in me because the
architecture is so remote and otherwordly. Perhaps my
career as an art critic began at the moment I saw the
holy card, which had a baroque warmth that the city
itself did not possess. I loved the luminescence of holy
cards, their gold and silver foil papers surrounding the
saints in their humbler, more subdued colours. They
looked so real that I believed if I popped them out of
their laminated packets, the saints themselves would
spring out at me and perform any miracle I requested of
them. I remember gazing longingly at the huge collection of them and trying to decide which ones I could
purchase. Mostly because I still have a postcard of it, I
also remember all too clearly the famous statue of the
little pissing boy, called the Mannekin-Pis, who is
supposed to have extinguished by "watering" a fire-
cracker meant to blow up the town hall. Other legends
had it that he was the son of a rich bourgeois, found by
his grateful parents at the corner of the rue de l'Étuve
and the rue du Chêne, relieving himself in the same
manner as the famous fountain. It has become a symbol

of all the city's tragedies and fortunes. I think of it when I recall the grubby street urchins who played on the paving stones outside the church, and wonder if their parents would have even sent out a search party should news of their children's disappearance be made known. I think of the miracle of the fountain's survival, its mocking and arrogant arc of water spouting into the air, when I sift through the sepia-toned photographs of rubble-strewn postwar cities.

But it was really the holy card I finally selected at St. Catherine's church that captured my most intense memory of Brussels. We went to church early that evening. I collected holy cards for my missal from every church I visited with my parents. Some of these I traded with other girls from my catechism class. For many years of Sundays after that day, I remained enamoured of the gilded picture I bought with my allowance at the gift shop at St. Catherine's in Brussels, a fourteenth-century church rebuilt in 1850. It was a version of the Assumption that I eventually learned was attributed to that "meticulous Flemish realist" who alone succeeded in "unifying myth and reality," Rubens. I remember being astounded by the pull between heaven and earth, the voluptuous virgin, the brilliant darkness, so much muscular light and glory.

On the back of the card was written mysteriously: *Expleto terrestris vitae cursu.* My fifth-grade Latin teacher, a Jesuit, later explained it to me as: "The Immaculate

Mother of God, the ever-Virgin Mary, having completed the course of her earthly life, was assumed body and soul into heavenly glory." (Much too lugubrious. I have always preferred the compactness of Latin.) He went on to explain the official Church doctrine on Mary's privileged role as daughter, spouse and mother; as Adam's love for Eve led him into sin, so Christ's love for Mary led Him to allow her to share in the conflict. This escaped me entirely, and made me sorry I'd asked, especially since I doubted the veracity of his translation. My favourite features of the holy card were the rays of gold emanating from Mary's soaring arms as she rose toward heaven. I returned my eyes again and again to the Rubens and was swept up into the unending white light.

My parents must also have loved blinding white light because they became snowbirds and settled in Florida when my father retired, where they assumed that the sun would keep them eternally young. My father also assumed that happiness was something that could be bought or achieved if he just found the magic formula; he never learned that happiness is not a permanent condition, but a relative state, a matter of degree. I have had my share of assumptions, too. For one thing, I always assumed that I too could fly. Indeed, in my dreams I flew all the time, and had difficulty accepting the reality that, if I stood on the edge of some cliff, I should not be able to take off with the same ease I did in those dreams. I assumed I would always be as ugly as my father informed

me I was, and did not assume I had the right to be beautiful. I had also assumed that my lifelong argument with
God about what was fair and what was not, begun that
spring in Brussels, would go on forever and forever, and I
had planned on winning. I had *not* assumed that I would
be left here, standing alone, shouting in the dark.

．ﾉ

MY FATHER COMMITTED SUICIDE LAST TUESDAY
night. My youngest sister Francine, who had stayed in
touch with my parents many years longer than I cared
to, called to tell me the news, and to ask whether or not
I wanted to attend the funeral. At first she told me it was
only one funeral. I had not spoken to my father in eight
years, not since he had rearranged the fine bones of my
mother's face beyond recognition, the year before they
retired to Florida. I tried to picture her again, smiling in
the Jackie Kennedy suit, how proud she had been of it,
but all I could think of was her bandaged head in the
hospital, how even her tears couldn't escape the eye slits
carved in the plaster covering her mummified face. My
sister announced that my parents had been reading
Romeo and Juliet the week before their deaths, that my
mother had called to tell her that she was newly enamoured of Shakespeare. This was her way of preparing me
for the fact that there were two funerals. I cannot envision what demons my father grappled with as he lay in
that white room in a Miami condo, curled up in a fetal

position, nor can I guess what memories haunted him as he clutched the same weapon he had used to kill my mother several hours earlier. Perhaps he cried afterward, not for her, but for himself. Human beings are rarely given to understand what occurs between them in the darkness. Most of us recover by mourning; others encounter only the madness. *Let us have grace*, then.

My father still stands in my mind, young, dignified and handsome, raised halfway up the staircase that leads to a small restaurant in Brussels. He is wearing his RCAF uniform, the distressed leather jacket covering his wings, its brown softness and fine fissures gleaming in the light from the open window on the landing. It is a weak spring light, but gentle somehow, barely illuminating his face and changing his otherwise invisible eyelashes into a startling, haloed fringe around eyes that are sad and hungry; I am condemned to see those eyes every morning in my mirror. I do look at myself in the mirror now, and I know that I am not ugly. But when I look back carefully at that scene in Brussels, I see that he stands there, poised in flight, one leg up on the next stair, bent over so that he can extend one arm down toward me as I climb upward, beckoning. The staircase below is only dimly lit, and outside the sun is descending slowly over the evening. It is an indeterminate season; the ground is still damp with winter's cold breath but musty with the warmer odours of packed dirt, stale beer, urine. Fog swirls around the building, the streets are paved with sombre concrete and cracked cobblestones, the vendors are closing their stalls now, and the ghosts of incomplete conversations linger in empty alleyways. Looking down upon that edifice, the first thing I notice is that the roof is flat, but as I rise higher and higher, that it is surrounded by a certain lustre. Drawing back, pulling away, my hand on the throttle of the engine of a Lancaster Mark II bomber, I stare down upon the tiny city of Brussels in the expanding dark night. The smaller it grows in the distance, the greater my compulsion to recall the erosion of an embattled Europe. Others could be forgiven if they believed that all that could be seen in that evolving twilight beneath them was one city twinkling its neon-lit eyes at them, or if it appeared to them that thousands of tiny white votive tapers were being lit to usher in the blackening night. But I know, God knows, and my father knows, that these are young, tender, white asparagus shoots. And they are everywhere, luminous, just below the surface of the earth, reaching toward the sky.

Blue Moon

"A BLUE MOON IS A MISPERCEPTION," RAY announces. "There is no such thing as a blue moon." He and Holly are sitting around the campfire circle with Cathy and Rick, the second night of their annual pilgrimage to Kanaka Lake, undertaken without their children, cookstove or electricity. Things must be kept simple. Ray is also adamant about silence, especially in the mornings. At home Holly is not supposed to put on lights until his eyes have had at least an hour to adjust. He is more at ease out in the woods, where there are no fluorescent lights. They have rented this campsite for eight years in a row. Soon it will be dark and someone will have to build the fire. Last summer they decided to add the ghetto blaster to their list of urban relics better left behind, so they could hear the silence more completely.

Ray is a tall man whose blood does not reach all his extremities; he always rubs his cold feet under her backside when they zip their sleeping bags together to sleep in the tent. It may be this that has been destroying Holly. Many years ago Ray had wooed her with his warm wit, but later she realized that he only brought that out for show. In fact, it was annexed to his heart like a starlit sky into which he led her to see all its vitality. Still later, he led her into his real darkness, where no stars shone. She felt tiny and shivering, alone in a cavernous black sky that arched menacingly over her. He was the solid ground, the scientist, and she was the flighty art student; these were the myths they had invented to sustain eleven years of marriage.

Rick gathers all the kindling and sets it down against the largest rock outlining the campfire. He kicks idly at the ashes, moving the charred wood pieces away from the centre with the toe of his construction boot. He looks wan, restless. His long hair is tucked under a baseball cap, which he removes ceremoniously, bowing toward Holly.

"*Voilà, madame.* The rest is all yours." He sits down on a log to watch her, pulling out a plastic bag and his rolling papers. Rick shakes the marijuana onto a nearby *Rolling Stone*, and scrapes it toward the centre with the cardboard from the Vogue papers. He is lost in thought.

Holly begins constructing a miniature log cabin, the kindling in the centre, remembering the way she'd been instructed to build it when she was in Guides. It is the

first time she has attempted to build the fire; usually this
is Ray's job. Ray strides over and knocks the log cabin
down with one sweep of his large hand.

"You're never going to get a fire going like that. Was this
some Girl Guide badge you earned for pretty fire designs?
What is it with girls and fires, anyway?" He smirks in the
direction of Cathy, who is gathering more wood along
the shore. Smiling, she hands her bundle over to him, and
he grins back. As abruptly as he drops the subject of the
blue moon, Ray releases the bundle inside the circle of
stones. He takes the longer branches and breaks them over
his knee with loud snapping noises. Rick lifts his head to
watch the two of them. Then he goes back to putting a
balled-up bit of cardboard into the end of the joint, his
homemade version of a cigarette filter.

Holly is slow to respond. "Actually, it *is* something I
learned in Guides. And we had to make sure they worked,
too." She feels her cheeks growing warm, although she does
her best not to let his comments get her agitated. She
won't let him win again. "Just practising the Guide motto:
'Be helpful to others.'" She makes a joke of it. Let him
think she was just getting the wood ready for him.

As quickly as Ray gets the fire going, she puts the
scene from her mind. These are their holidays, after all,
and she isn't going to let anything Ray says get to her.
Her thoughts drift back to the previous night. Cocooned
in her sleeping bag, listening to the waves, she slid across
her Thermarest and reached over to stroke the back of

Ray's neck with her fingers. He would spurn her again, as usual. She wanted to memorize the nape of his neck, catalogue it for future reference.

"Look, forget it. I'm beat, okay?" Why had he assumed that she only wanted to make love? What was wrong with her just stroking him, maybe wanting to be stroked back in return? She had rolled over, releasing a sigh from the Thermarest. There was no point in going over old territory. Ray claimed that her need for affection was excessive, abnormal.

"You must be premenstrual or you wouldn't be so oversensitive," he'd said, just as she was drifting off to sleep. Ray believes in a rational world, in answers that are clear and simple and problems that can be diagnosed and solved. "It isn't anything personal," he'd reminded her, softening his tone a little.

But today she thinks it *is* personal. It's been so long since he has touched her. Still, maybe she is being irritable. He'd done most of the driving to get here, so he probably was exhausted. But her anger does not subside, only mellows a little, as she listens to him pontificating to Cathy and Rick about the goddamn moon again.

⌒

CATHY IS FLICKING FRAGMENTS OF PINE CONE into flames that lick them up eagerly and emit sharp crackles. She gathers her long hair into a ponytail and wraps it, tucking in the end, then lets it fall loosely on her shoulders until it springs free and drapes at the sides of her oval face; she does this over and over. Holly watches Ray's face as it remains fixed on Cathy's hair; she is intrigued by the way his skin glows in the firelight. Turning to the fire, she sees red and orange tongues leap higher before she looks back up at the moon. Little wings of fire emblazon themselves on her irises before she takes in the dark. He's right. The moon's not blue, it's actually green now.

And of course he's still talking about the moon, won't shut up about it, even as he bends over to put a stick on the fire. The flames rise upward, quickly. "Not only is the moon not actually blue, but it's not even blue as in 'rare.' It's just too common, astronomically speaking," he goes on. "There are two full moons in a calendar month as often as every three years." Holly remembers that this was what initially attracted her to Ray — this precision from him, the way he could pinpoint exactly what was going on. She believed that it rooted her, placed her on the map. She expects him to lift his telescope out of the trunk at any moment and shoulder it toward the clearing by the beach, away from the heat of the fire. Perhaps Cathy will carry the roll of charts and the logbooks Ray is so fond of recording his observations in. Holly is dazzled by his ability to name the heavens. He has some good qualities that offset how stubborn he can be. The beans and pork smell good enough to eat. So they do eat, as ravenously as they always do when they're outdoors.

Cathy has brought homemade salsa and rips open a bag of corn chips that she passes around.

"What you are seeing is actually a cloud beside the moon, lit up by the setting sun," Ray remarks. Holly knows her eye is often fooled by bright red lights, especially in the city. She remembers staring at the sun as a girl, then squeezing her eyes shut to luxuriate in the gold burst behind her eyelids. She chews her corn chip slowly. Ray holds out a marshmallow on a stick to her, but he's charred it, it's black and puffy. She shakes her head, so he offers it to the others. Cathy turns her eyes up at him so that, briefly, the fire is reflected in her pupils; she extends her hand toward the oozing marshmallow. She pulls it slowly off the stick and slides it into her mouth. Ray watches Cathy swallow, turns his face away for a moment, then plants his feet on the ground and pulls his tall frame unsteadily into an upright position. It must be stargazing time. They will follow him toward the beach, as they always do. Holly is reaching for a twist tie to seal up the marshmallow bag, but cannot leave the reflected warmth of the fire just yet. Rick is wiping up the last of the salsa with a crust of bread, and singing "Tupelo Honey" at the top of his voice. Holly has known him for years, long before she met Ray, and cannot remember a time when he did not sing.

Cathy says, "Let's just leave the dishes until the morning. I'll rinse off the grease with sand, and maybe one of you guys could get rid of the garbage so the bears don't get into it. Remember last year." She giggles as she picks up her book from the log where she left it earlier. Cathy's been naming the constellations to all of them tonight, describing the meteorite shower due around 1:20 in the morning. She says she's found the constellation of Hercules, now visible in the sky, in her *Guide to the Galaxy*, and is looking up the name of the most prominent of its stars. "Look, I found it, that must be Rasalgethi," she says to Ray, pronouncing the word with difficulty and looking at him as he nods in approval. "It's Arabic for 'head of the kneeling one.' This book is amazing!"

Once Holly had cared enough to impress Ray to look things up, to please him, to flatter him so that he could congratulate her for being a quick learner. Stretching up and pointing at the star, Cathy looks taller than Holly remembers, possibly even slimmer. She is animated, happier than last summer. Last summer the two of them had become so close, sharing mutual disappointments in their careers, wondering how they'd become middle-aged and compromised in their goals. She and Cathy had stayed up one night after the guys had gone to bed, opened a bottle of cognac, and poured their hearts out to one another as easily as they poured the fiery liquid into their enamelled tin cups. But the past year of bickering between Holly and Ray has eroded all of Holly's confidence. She remembers Cathy looking at her and saying, "You are so lucky to have Ray. He's so together and interested in the world around him. Rick gets so caught up in himself that I feel like I don't exist for him anymore."

How can Holly share with Cathy the distance she feels from Ray lately? The obsessive way Holly wonders what her life would have been like had she not married him? Cathy knows nothing about his small cruelties; she doesn't have to live with him every day. Holly yawns, doesn't think she can stay up late enough for the meteorites. Still, her eyes are drawn to the sky. Too early yet. It's not that she isn't greedy for the touch of the stars. Only that she never cared to understand them too much. Or so she tells herself.

Holly hears zippers scrape and halt, and knows that Rick has headed back to his tent. Then he returns to the campfire, leans his guitar case against the log, in preparation for their singing later. After all these years, the four of them have quite the repertoire of songs. He slips his red lumberjack shirt on over his T-shirt.

"Short walk to the dump?" he asks. Holly realizes he's addressing her. Lately she feels bewildered, as if she's living on some other planet, unable to communicate with the human beings in her life. She resents carrying their trash to the dump each night, but the government cutbacks have affected maintenance at all provincial parks. There is no longer a bright-eyed kid whose summer job it is to arrive with a pickup every day, to clean out the trash bins, and to haul away the stinking garbage bags. Getting to her feet, she follows Rick up the sandbank, stumbling over large stones and broken logs, angling her feet sideways for traction, until both of them have reached the pine floor of the forest above the beach. Here the smell of the lake is sharp, nearly brackish. The air feels tender, tentative, as if something is slipping away, replaced by an atmosphere that is bracing, expansive. The scent of Rick's skin is keen to her nose. It's really dark now that they've pulled away from the beach. Twigs rattle crisply under Holly's hiking boots. They stop in unison on the edge of the woods, listening to the new silence. Now that her eyes surrender to the blackness, stripped of fireglow, speculative patterns emerge among the branches. It's as if they are both listening for some signal.

The trees are suddenly dense and massive as Holly and Rick resume their saunter, moving quietly, Holly a few paces behind Rick. He holds back an overhanging limb until she catches up with him; he lowers it back in place when Holly passes in front of him. Then he is beside her, their paces matched. Their shoulders brush and he pulls away, as if she has accidentally given him an electric shock, just as Holly feels a small quivering in her legs. She cannot explain to herself why she should feel so jittery at such a slight touch, nor can she find anything light to say. The silence is overwhelming, and she wonders when one of them will break it. Finally, just when Holly is afraid that he might touch her again, Rick speaks.

"You seem far away lately," he ventures.

"Just tired. It's been a stressful week and —"

"Yeah. Ray looks beat too."

"No, at work, I mean. It's, um —"

"Oh."

Rick seems embarrassed at having misunderstood her, and she feels confused too. She wants to rescue him, so she tries again, although she is reluctant to talk, unwilling to dispel whatever has descended over them. Her lips tremble.

"It's just that we have a new manager, and he's been really lording it over everybody lately. It gets a little hard to take. So right now I'm trying not to think about work or anything."

They walk along a little further. Conversation between them has never been this strained before. Rick is usually in a joking mood. Holly likes his wit, the way he makes her tremble with laughter, piling one silliness on top of another until all of them erupt in hysterics. They'd always enjoyed this banter, this give and take, she muses. She remembers one summer he came to visit her when she was still in school in Kingston. They sat on her verandah drinking Campari, talking about their debts, about academic pretension, about aspirations. Ray was in Red Lake, working, and Holly was counting on him being home in time for the weekend so the three of them could go out for dinner. But by Saturday afternoon, exhausted by cycling, Rick and Holly were restless and hungry and Ray was nowhere in sight. From her costume chest she'd dragged

out a black lace dress, Rick had put on his good trousers
and they had taken the ferry across to Wolfe Island.

She can no longer remember what they ate, only that
they drank and talked until late, and caught the last
ferry back across the lake. Standing beside Rick on the
deck, Holly felt the ferry engine churning below her feet.
She realized suddenly that she was happy. Above her the
glimmering stars were soft and spoke of mysterious
vignettes. Up there among the heavenly bodies hung her
uncompromised heart, an entire galaxy. The air was deliciously complicated too, as if it promised layers of possible
meaning. Or maybe it's just nostalgia, she thinks now.
What happened to that lightness?

Now they are solemn, awkward. It is not an occasion
for joking or being lighthearted. They have been walking in
silence, and have covered a lot of ground without her
having realized it. What could she possibly say? Would he
care that she and Ray have not made love for months? She
could never ask him how frequently he and Cathy did,
whether they were still in love. They are nearing the large
piles of trash ahead. The dump smells fetid. Rick heaves
the green garbage bag over the top edge of the dumpster.
The fluorescent lights around the garbage bins cast a
warm glow. He shifts toward her and she finds his face
directly in front of hers. She is not sure what she is
looking for in his face, but suddenly she feels herself
growing heated. His arms are well developed and muscular
under his T-shirt, and this sudden knowledge makes her

blush. Why has she never looked at him this carefully and closely before? Holly spins around quickly before he has a chance to register her panic.

"We'd better get back," she mutters, cursing herself inwardly. Why should they have to hurry back? She is making no sense at all, no matter what she says. Better just to shut up. Rick also turns around abruptly and they both start walking back toward the campsite. Their strides are evenly matched; she likes his rhythm and their synchronized breathing.

"Looks like we'll have good weather while we're here, anyway." Why does he have to spoil this moment with talking? She places one foot in front of the other with an orderliness that she remembers from schoolyards.

"So, what's really going on with you?" he ventures.

"I don't know what you mean."

He exhales and sighs. "It's just that you're pretending everything is fine all the time."

"Well, it is. Anyway, I'm an optimist." Teeth gritted. He's presuming too much.

"Look, you haven't exactly been happy the last couple of years. What am I supposed to do, just ignore it? I mean, I've kept my comments to myself. But you really —"

Holly tunes him out. It's relentless, this line of pursuit, and disloyal too. She wants her summer holidays by the lake to be filled with shimmering decencies so she can go home and count her blessings. Furious, she picks up her pace and marches ahead of him.

Last week when she was packing for the trip, she had felt some brightness seize her. As if the act of filling the cooler and planning their camping meals had meant something was shifting in her ordinary life. Was it just anticipation? Or that the days were still long, that light stayed well into the evening? It was as if the tremor of summertime she remembered when she was a girl were rippling through her body again. The sort of delight she felt when the outdoor swimming pool opened for the first time of the season and, shivering, she came out of the water feeling buoyant. She had told Ray about this once, and he had nodded in understanding. They hadn't needed words then. She and Ray had often swum together in the river years ago, then warmed each other under the same towel on the bank.

Their steps have slowed, and Holly feels sand slipping under her boots once more. She can make out the outline of the campsite and the appearance of the others, who are now within hearing distance. End of attempted pep talk, she thinks with relief. She jumps down onto the sandbank eagerly, moves forward toward the telescope Ray has erected on the beach. She can't see his eyes, in fact his whole face is obscured, but she can tell he is squinting. In silhouette, he appears gentle, gawky.

"Come quickly," he says. "The shower will start over there." He pulls her, too hard, by the wrist, and points upward. When he's agitated, he's always like this. And Holly forgives him his clumsiness. Tonight he seems

particularly nervous; his hands shake as he turns the telescope lens. She wonders now at her sudden tenderness
toward him as she sees him hunched over the telescope,
his large shoulder blades folded like wings, the back of
his shaved neck exposed. Wonders especially since all she
has felt lately is rage, wanting to punish him for his with-
drawal from her. Her stomach lurches; she tastes the
beans and rice she ate at supper, as she moves quickly
alongside the others. They are lined up, the four of them,
on the beach, as if waiting for a miracle to happen.

THE STARS ARE ALL THERE, IN ORDER, AS EXPECTED.
Cathy shivers, pulls her cardigan tightly around her
shoulders, and hugs her arms.

"I am so excited about this!" she exclaims. "Remember
the bunch of shooting stars that exploded all at the
same time?" she asks, turning toward Ray, who nods
distractedly. "Look, isn't that Venus?" Cathy points to
the sky. She pulls her hair into a rope and shakes it out
along her back, arching her neck to look upward. Rick
follows her finger.

Holly does look above at the inky cosmos, but she
cannot focus. She feels her eyes welling over with tears.
She fears that Cathy, who has moved beside her, will ask
why. Holly turns her face away, unable to speak. She
walks toward the tent and unlaces her hiking boots,

peels off her socks and slides her feet into her sandals. The rest of her friends settle on a log near the firepit.

Everyone gazes in awe at the sky, mesmerized, while time seems to run out. She can see shooting stars — one, then two more in quick succession. Now it seems that shooting stars mock her hopes. Like the old Norse myths she read where meteors herald pain and disaster for humankind, demanding sacrifice as propitiation. The quiet is chilling now, as if everyone is frozen, posing for a photographer who wants to capture this moment in time. The way we were, she thinks. It feels like we will all be here forever, just waiting. Yet the stars in a milky, blinking swirl glitter constantly. Perhaps they do augur something hopeful after all.

Rick is the first to break away. He sits by the fire again, and begins strumming the guitar, tuning the strings, then strumming again. When he finally starts to play, Holly is instantly alert to the rush, as if a slow guitar lick could alter the course of the world. There is a tingling along the back of her neck as she turns around and walks toward him. She watches his hands move, and she realizes that she has memorized all the hairs along the backs of his hands, the slender fingers. She imagines trusting her breasts to those hands, then brushes the thought away. Swallows hard. Wills herself back from her reverie. Locates herself standing calmly on the ground, her rightful place, subdued and surprised.

It is not true that she knows nothing about heavenly
bodies. She remembers now in exact detail what she
learned from Ray about the moon. She had been proud of
the way that Ray had taught them all the particulars
about astronomy, proud of his memory for scientific
detail. Especially since it contrasted so sharply with his
inability to remember details of a more personal kind.
Especially since he communicated about so little else.
Why has she been mute all these years? And suppressed
all the details that she remembers in their painful
clarity? Like this: his hands retreating from her when
she reached for him. Like this: his back turning to her
when she cried. And what about the things she has to
teach him? The things she remembers best?

Like this: on very rare occasions, she remembers, the
moon has a bluish tinge. Only after a violent volcanic
eruption, or a big forest fire. Particles from volcanic dust,
or smoke, can be the perfect size to scatter light prefer-
entially in the red. Your eyes are left with an excess of
blue light in the moon's image. Maybe it might damage
your eyes if you stare at it too long. Or maybe you just
open them to something completely different. She could
teach him that. That kind of seeing excites her.

A blue moon. The unforeseen. The heavens hold a
certain possibility tonight, Holly thinks.

The Way Home

THE WAY BACK HOME ALWAYS SEEMS LONGER. The signs all changed by the absence of light, and we're tired, drawn by the swishing of windshield wipers into reverie. All of our energy has been expended in the more frenzied moments of the party before midnight; then we fold ourselves back into the fatigue of familiar shapes. He has offered Candace a ride home, and she occupies the back seat of the car, nervously trying to fill the space that lingers between our pauses. She is describing the delicious sensation of being lulled to sleep as a child on nights just such as these, long winding journeys into the fleecy white landscape. Snowflakes hurling themselves against the windshield, the engine humming beneath the flannel-covered limbs of her brothers and herself, huddled on the back seat as her parents drove them home in animated silence. "How comforting it was," she exclaims. To be wrapped in the eiderdown lightness of streetlamps flashing by in regular geometric patterns on the rear car window. How soothing to be rocked to sleep by the steady rhythm of cars zooming by in the opposite lane, the familiar droning crescendo and diminuendo of rubber tire singing against wet pavement. The soft click of the car heater, the somnolent warmth gradually engulfing her child's mind that, though it vowed to stay awake to take it all in, gratefully succumbed to slumber with no further protest. To surrender to the knowledge that someone strong and large would gently shift the weight of her child's body and carry her indoors at last, only briefly interrupting a deep, abiding sleep that took her to other faraway places.

I am listening to her reminisce like this, and I feel a sudden pang just above my diaphragm. For although I can imagine that kind of security and warmth, although it appeals to me the way illustrated children's tales do, I cannot fathom what such knowledge implies, am leery, listening to inconsistent notes, cynically hungering for contradictions. The alcohol in my blood resurges in a jolt of anger. I fume in silence, distract myself by pushing back my cuticles. I too remember the late night drives home with my parents, huddled with my sisters on the upholstered back seat, pillow clutched against belly, wrapped in terror at my father's erratic driving. My mother would have begged him earlier not to drive until he was sober, but he would charm her into believing he was in control, and so we would set off on our perilous voyage into the night. Exclaiming loudly, pronouncing judgement on the behaviour of various relatives we had visited that evening, he would punctuate his speech with wide Gallic gestures that caused his hands to fly from the wheel, forced my breath into the back of my throat. I would make gentle cooing noises to my sisters in the back: Nicole, who was crying in fear, and Suzanne, whose alabaster face masked confusion. My mother would sit in numbness, knowing that any interruption of my father's soliloquy could result in another collision. To say nothing of the lawsuit that he incurred after crippling a young boy on a bicycle. By the time we were all falling into bed, my jaw would be clenched, my knuckles white, grateful. I never slept on these journeys.

Tonight it is the same. Already my teeth ache. After we drop Candace off, silence throbs in my skull. He is trying to reach me, making small talk, but in my wretchedness I find his voice grates more than comforts. So we turn on the radio, an exaggerated listening takes hold of us, and we drift into different spheres. For me it is trying to recall where I was when this Beatles song was released, catapulting backwards over ancient memories. Then we are overtaken by the deep tones of Stan Rogers, whose voice inspires him: "When you're listening to him, it's like being rocked to sleep in your daddy's arms," he says. I need air, I am already reaching for the door latch before he can slow the car down to let me out. He believes I am going to be ill. I don't give a damn what he thinks. I am running, my thin leather boots unable to hold back the chill of the snowbanks. My lungs hurt from the coldness of air, and my anger fuels the crazy jagged path I cut through crusted snow, beyond the ditch and deep into the wood. I keep running until the trees open onto a field of undulating snowbanks, smooth and gentle. But the rush in my veins is not easily appeased; it seeks its own edge, and tonight I am too hard to handle, even for me.

Finally it subsides, though my mind is still racing. I have left the car far behind me on the highway. The sharp cold darkness requires that I immediately shift my senses, no chance to make transitions. Engulfed by a black expansiveness, too bracing and stark in its totality, I collapse into a snowdrift. Sounds of cars are like distant waves. I am left with only this merciless blue whiteness, where every small noise nearby produces a pronounced snap. My heart pounds furiously. I hear the car door bang in the far distance of the other world I left behind. My toes are so cold they send heat waves up my legs. I pinch myself to get my blood circulating, to reassure myself I am real. I am that far away.

He approaches slowly, deliberately, registering his presence and his incomprehension wordlessly. He moves alongside me on the snowbank, lying down. His stillness makes me shiver. I close my eyes, but so much remains fugitive, interior, unreachable.

Light is filling the sky against my will. Snowflakes descend gracefully, large and soft and mute. How could I have been oblivious to their weight falling all around me? It seems that hours have passed. Galaxies of flakes close out the immobile sky. I am sinking, shocking heaviness, pulled into the contours of the ground on which I lie, the snow building a beautiful emptying bowl around my angel limbs. My arms and legs flap back and forth, just to shift the shapes filling my hollows.

Beneath me, shuddering networks of roots and delicate fronds reach upward, defining their spiked boundaries. Underground foliage assumes detailed proportion, arching, dignified, knowing. In the accumulating dark, light from the centre of the earth strains, creeps forward, like mortar filling cracks, until it gains power, groping branches that scrape the stars. Light continues to expand upward. The cells of our bodies are at last spoken by gravity. Someday soon we will be replaced, marrow by silt, but at the core of this earth, there is still room for us.

Soon I will peel off the blanket of the sky, hands locked in suspension against cobalt. Later I will reach for him, our bones compelled to recognize each other through layers and layers of concealing flesh, seeking confirmation. I will be drawn into every pore, every wisp, each fibre responding to the running path of blood that travels between us. But for the moment, my eye swallows the seam between horizon and hill, folds of snow embracing us. Standing up slowly, I see how swiftly our bowls in the snowbank, the cavities that held our bodies, resume their ancient shapes as snow gathers them together, erasing our impressions. By sunrise there will be no trace of our having occupied this moment, save the lightness where our wings swept the surface of the snow.

Sister Marguerite

THE IDEAL OF RELIGIOUS COMMITMENT. I SEE NOW that that is what Sister Marguerite struggled for all her life, and what I am certain she was trying to instill in me. At the age of twelve, however, I scorned such piety, preferring instead to play hooky with the other girls I had persuaded to skip classes with me. We jammed our packages of smokes into the already bulging pockets of our blazers. Kicking off our heavy black oxfords into the depths of our lockers, we exchanged them for platform shoes or dangerously high heels, and then stumbled defiantly in the direction of downtown. By the time we had reached the bridge and were certain to be beyond the sighting range of any nun who happened to be out walking or following the path to the Grotto to pray to the Virgin, we had rolled up the waistbands of our kilts so that they no longer hung at the regulation length of two inches above the knee, but might pass for rather bulky miniskirts.

Once on the main drag, we found the usual hangout, and filled our favourite booth at the Milano Steakhouse, a dimly lit restaurant where we were greeted by squeaky red Naugahyde seats, gold wallpaper festooned with swirling black velvet patterns, and, most importantly, where the squat, swarthy and unscrupulous owner, eager for afternoon clientele, never requested ID. Thinking ourselves terribly sophisticated and immune to catastrophe, we would order rounds of green grasshoppers and get slowly tipsy and giggly on crème de menthe. It astonishes me now that we did not order pink ladies, or one of the other concoctions illustrated on the paper table mats that consumed our attention, although we memorized how many ounces of spirits and other ingredients were contained in each of those drinks with the diligence of examinants, believing this to be essential knowledge for our future lives. That we should insist on green drinks after the oppressive daily sight of hundreds of girls clad in the same green blazers, green plaid kilts and green tights suggests a conformity that we claimed to despise but that crept into our bloodstream, absorbed as easily as alcohol.

During these excursions, I convinced myself that I was happy, ecstatically and drunkenly alive. As the ringleader of the group, the last thing on my mind was what my English teacher was attempting to pass on to me or any of her other students. All the catechistic recitations of Shakespeare or Dante that may have momentarily impressed me earlier in the day evaporated in the glorious haze of my newfound camaraderie, seemed paltry compared to learning from my girlfriends how to blow perfect smoke rings that spiralled heavenward from my upturned mouth. Of the greatest significance was developing our conspiracy to escape the restaurant without paying the bill; we planned to slip down the stairs, ostensibly in search of the john, but actually to rush through the kitchen door and out into the alley after evading the cook, while the last girl simultaneously distracted the hostess. Surprisingly, this ruse had worked several times, only because the restaurant manager was often in the back room, chatting with his cronies and smoking cigars, and a series of assistant managers failed to recognize us for who we were. It was miraculous that no one ever came running after us in the alley, brandishing a meat cleaver. We were impervious to danger, mocked all authority, taunted any man who told us what to do with obscenities that would have given any nun an apoplectic fit.

I do remember distinctly the first time Sister Marguerite introduced us to John Donne. It was early in the spring, damp, the sun flashing through the windows only intermittently. I was daydreaming as usual, staring out the window at the minute tufts of grass that sprouted sporadically from the cracked earth, and at the winding runnels of water that pushed themselves forward with a viscous insistency, only to diminish to trickles and then be absorbed by parched dirt halfway along their journey. The sun glared brightly on the newest puddle of water, metamorphosing it temporarily to quicksilver, and then darkened just as rapidly. Free from external distractions then, I listened with renewed intensity.

She began by reading from Donne's sermons, and then moved on to the satire on religion. We were scandalized. In the satire was a contempt for religion that I recognized as my own, a desire for certainty that no priest, expounding on doctrine, could assuage. She gripped the book tightly, her free hand fluttering nervously as she read, while her head bobbed up and down excitedly. Occasionally she would lift her head to speak directly to us, peering above her bifocals, to explain the context of a particular word whose meaning had long since been altered. When she finally arrived at the poetry, her right foot began to tap out the rhythm and her enthusiasm frightened me, convinced as I was that she was in the grip of some epileptic tremor. Older girls in the upper classes had warned us of her erratic behaviour, and the stories of her eccentricities were circulated after "lights out" with as much glee as stolen chocolate bars. Watching her now, her wimple flapping and the crucifix slapping methodically against the cardboard stiffness of the starched white bib she wore like plated armour, I felt certain that at any moment her feet would levitate from the ground, in an imitation of the Ascension. Or that the wimple she wore would transmute into wings, and she would be off like the Flying Nun. Her nostrils

flared, her eyes widened and her enunciation grew clearer
as she read from the poem called "A Valediction: Forbidding
Mourning":

> Our two souls therefore, which are one,
> Though I must go, endure not yet
> A breach, but an expansion,
> Like gold to airy thinness beat.

One soul travels in a wide circle, while the other remains
in one place, yet both are linked together even as the arc of
the circle widens, she explained. Like a compass, she said.
I felt my heart quickening, pounding like a fist behind my
rib cage as she finished reading. Turning abruptly on her
heels to face us, Sister Marguerite expanded on the concept
of metaphysical wit, describing how conceits placed strains
upon the intellect. We tittered at the word "conceit." As
she demonstrated with the compass on the palm of her
outstretched hand, seemingly incongruous words and
objects spoke of love with a clarity that was instantly and
shockingly apparent to me. The class ended too quickly, so
that I felt weakened, stunned and awkward, completely at
a loss for the usual sarcastic commentary I would mutter to
the other girls as we moved into the corridor. I paused at
the blackboard, which Sister was wiping energetically, and
caught the dark scent of myrrh emanating from her black
robe before the chalk dust tickled my nose.

Nervously I asked her about the compass. About Donne.

About the titles of some of the poems she had recited. Her face beamed and her eyes glistened as she spoke; all I remember is that she promised to bring me more books on metaphysical poetry the following Monday. The rest of the day seemed prosaic and stolid, and Monday was light years away.

The weekend was excruciatingly long. The heavy spring rains increased in ferocity. Only late on Sunday afternoon was there even a hint of sunshine, but it pressed itself dramatically upon the remaining day, silhouetting the lining of the heavy drapery in our dorm. For once I could not wait until classes began. Matins dragged on and on, and then came the mass, the ancient priest's gnarled hands raising the host in what I took to be a deliberate and exaggerated slowness, as if to emphasize the inappropriateness of my impatience. Every day at mass I found myself in a kind of trance. Halfway through communion, the sun woke up, its rays pushing beseechingly through the stained-glass windows. Kneeling quickly, I waited for the chalice to reach my lips, for the stale wafer to melt on my tongue, its unsatisfying flatness inspiring my stomach with anticipation for the hot breakfast awaiting me in half an hour in the refectory. All morning, the hours plodded slowly by, oblivious to the strain of sunlight against the shadows fanning the courtyard onto which all our classrooms faced. When English finally commenced at eleven, I was starving again, the first girl to reach her seat. I stared anxiously at Sister Marguerite's desk, but her heavy tomes and lecture notes, usually placed squarely in the centre of the podium, were nowhere in sight. By now the strong spring light spilled in checkerboard fashion across the floor, its heat intense. Sister Marguerite was late in entering the room, which should have alerted us immediately to the fact that something unusual was about to unfold. When we were finally seated and calm, Sister Marguerite paced back and forth, clearly agitated, almost as if she were in a trance. Then she turned to us with an uncharacteristically devilish grin.

"Class, I have decided that I am going to take you to the woods behind the convent. We will leave by the rear hallway door. Bring your notebooks, pencils and erasers. It is simply too fine a day to stay inside." We gasped, glanced at one another uncertainly, for this was so obvious an infraction of convent rules, which demanded that we remain indoors until four-thirty. Even then we were expected to submit ourselves by five-thirty for dinner. Most girls had music lessons during this interval, however, or played supervised sports, so unless we played hooky, our pale skin never saw the light of day. Walking in the woods was forbidden, unless a house nun accompanied us. When we did go to the woods, it was on stolen time, at night, to have a cigarette and exchange gossip. I had led many such nocturnal expeditions myself.

We were given time to run to our lockers and change our shoes, as Sister was adamant that we not ruin our good leather shoes. I slid on my sandals, even though she had

advised us to put on our gym shoes. Confused and recalci-
trant now, we marched in single file behind Sister
Marguerite. Reaching the edge of the grounds, past the
formal gardens and the statuary, we tramped along a path
where every raised root and undulation was familiar to us
by the light of our midnight torches, or the faint glow of
our cigarettes. In daylight now the path seemed oddly naked,
shorn of its sinister, gothic shadows. At last we reached
the knoll, where she commanded us to sit down, our shoes
muddy and our voices giddy. "Now, get out your pencils
and look at the sky. Look at these tiny green buds on all
these trees. Feel the new life beginning all around you, and
start to write. Just whatever comes into your head."

Sister Marguerite was balanced on her toes, her arms
gesticulating wildly as she spoke. She fluttered for a few
steps, and we thought she might either fly or fall, but then
she tugged at the rosary beads hanging from her waistband sash, and this seemed to restrain her, pull her toward
the ground. We were completely convinced that she was
indeed mad, and none of us made a move to open our
notebooks. Our giggling subsided, and for several moments
all we could do was blink in syncopation at the harsh light
surrounding us mercilessly from all sides. Accustomed to
the silence of the study hall, armed with copious research
material, we could write essays on prescribed topics or
translate dull Latin passages with relative ease. But no one
had ever commanded us to "just write whatever comes
into your heads," and we glanced nervously at one another

in penitent confusion. Robins darted from branch to branch, their trilling amplified by our unusual silence. For an eternity, I stared at the lunatic face of my English teacher, observed the grey hairs that darted out from behind the chalky cloth that gripped her jowls like mummified linen. Without her glasses, there was a startling weakness to her face, and in the unforgiving white light, her pallid visage wore a translucent sallowness that I had never noticed before. Our eyes made contact for a brief second, and I endured her scrutiny before I broke the stare. As she shifted her neck, I realized with sudden embarrassment that there was a tiny splash of freckles trailing across her nose, giving her face a peculiar but fleeting childishness.

And then, haltingly at first, but finally acting under some compulsion, I began to write. I kept writing for the next three days, and finally titled my composition, "An Inventory of Being." It was disjointed, sentimental and exuberant in its idealism, but it was all mine. I handed it in to Sister Marguerite, who kept it for an agonizingly long time. When she finally returned it to me three weeks later, an A in the upper corner, a remark in her flowery script graced it: "See the thumbtack marks on the page? That's where I pinned it on the sisters' bulletin board." I had never felt such pride before.

It was seven years later when I returned to the convent to visit Sister Marguerite, who had been forced to retire from teaching and now spent most of her days in the chapel. I was home for my sister's wedding, and decided to visit some of my old teachers at the convent before it was torn down and the nuns relocated to a retirement villa the following year; my mother had read the news of the closure in the newspaper and suggested that I might want to see some of the sisters. I thought of Sister Marguerite, who had not crossed my mind in those seven years. The relatively liberal papal doctrines of Vatican II had intervened in the time during which we had lost touch, and at first I did not recognize her without her veil. Her diminutive face was completely framed by white hair, and she appeared to resemble any ordinary old woman. Oddly this disappointed me, for I had never thought of nuns as women, masked as they were behind their black-and-white headdresses. As the Mother Superior led me to the waiting room, I took in more of Sister Marguerite's features: the tiny crows' feet spreading around her eyes, the dimples in her cheeks now deepened into wide furrows, the eyes themselves no longer sparkling. Her mouth seemed set. I could hardly imagine that this was the face that had launched an army of young girls toward literacy by delivering animated lectures.

I had so much to tell her. Now a second-year university student majoring in English, I was persuaded that I was learning everything there was to know about literature. I rattled off names and terms, trying to impress her with my erudition, hoping that she might remember that it was she who had first pierced my consciousness with a love of language. The eyes gave no response or recognition. She seemed saddened. Nervously I prattled on, discussing *Ulysses* excitedly, referring to the brilliance of its style, although in truth I had only managed the first few chapters before giving up in despair. There was a flicker in her eyes. "So you are reading Joyce?" she inquired slowly. She shook her head disapprovingly, and her fingers flicked at pieces of lint on her sleeve. "Such a misguided soul. He lost sight of our Saviour, you know." Then she regarded me curiously and a meanness I had not remembered stole into the corners of her eyes. "You always were one of the rebellious ones."

Afterwards our conversation leapt in different directions; she inquired about the health of a few of my former classmates, mentioned coyly the successful marriages of girls whose names I remembered only dimly, spoke of upcoming events in the parish. I left the convent that day with a new bitterness in my mouth, my head full of cynical expressions that an outdated sense of decorum prevented me from uttering in the presence of Sister Marguerite, and that would require several more years of reading to cultivate.

IT TOOK A LONG TIME FOR SISTER MARGUERITE to die. She lived to the shrivelled age of ninety-one, but I had long before put her out of my mind when I stumbled across the obituary this fall. I marvelled at the stock phrases contained in the saccharine, elegiac announcement, wondered whether she would really have sanctioned their conventionality or longed for some darker, more precise language. Now an English teacher myself, with a brood of children and a house that sprawls untidily in all directions, I rarely have time to shape words anymore. Yet here I am walking with the dog through the forest that borders our suburb, and I find myself groping after words with an obsessive devotion I believed had ceased to exist, imagining what it was I wanted to say to her on that long-ago occasion when I had visited her at the convent.

So absorbed am I in my search for refined phrases that I do not notice it immediately, only realize that my boots' rhythmic suction noises have been interrupted by the squishing sound of something less gripping than mud. In the dense shadows at the foot of the tree, it pokes upward, straining in a vulgar and insistent manner toward the light at the edge of the canopy of trees, its remarkable paleness offset by the deepening loam that encompasses it. Through the pine branches, a stream of thin liquid gold light pours upon the path, filtering dust and pollen and briefly illuminating a moist steam that rises from the ground.

Suddenly it is quite plainly visible. The variety is not one I am familiar with, though I pride myself on knowing my mushrooms. The white flesh of the gills and stem matches the tubes; the pores are also blanched, but the dry, yellowish brown cap is spotted on the top. At home later, I locate it in my field book and slowly chant the name to myself over and over: *Boletus affinus, Boletus affinus, Boletus affinus.* Commonly known as the spotted bolete. I hold the discovery to myself, its dark odour as mysterious as a secret.

Invert and Multiply

IT WAS HER VOICE THAT GAVE HER AWAY, EVEN though it had faded from the brassiness of childhood taunting to the husky voice of a woman who smoked and drank too much, even though Teresa's voice was now less resonant. The day that Jennifer heard it ringing out at The Maple Leaf Cafe, she felt not thirty-three but only twelve years old. She slid into a booth and opened up the *Maclean's* she was carrying in her purse. She'd intended to get to the bank, but that could wait, and it was lunch hour, the busiest ATM lineup time anyway.

From where she sat, Jennifer could look at the lunch counter without being noticed, in case it wasn't really Teresa. She ordered a coffee and a cold turkey sandwich. Teresa, if it was Teresa, sat chain-smoking at a swivel stool at the counter. Her teeth were now yellowish with stained, greying edges, and she was still wiry and nervous. Even from behind, Jennifer could see that Teresa was a little thinner but still possessed of the marvellous body by which she had earned her reputation. More alarming were the bruise marks along her arms and cheeks. How could Teresa have been hurt?

"It *is* you. I knew it!" Jennifer finally cried out. Teresa swivelled around on the red bar stool, leaning further forward from the hips, not certain if she were the one being addressed.

"Is that Jennifer Malone?" she said. Her fast-motion twirl in the chair reminded Jennifer of their dancing in the rec room when they were girls. How they had recruited Jennifer's older brother as the dance judge. Teresa had offered him a free show.

"It is indeed, you go-go girl," replied Jennifer, reverting to her childhood nickname. She was tempted to flap an imaginary little St. Martin's necktie and screech out the old fight song. Why? To prove her loyalty? We went to a goddamn Catholic school in a rough time and a rough neighbourhood, not some private girls' school like York House, she reminded herself. Teresa slid off the stool, came over to Jennifer's booth, and wrapped her in a swift embrace. She smelled of cigarette smoke, and after she let go of Jennifer, she returned to the counter to grab a package of Players Light and a Bic lighter in one hand and a half-filled ashtray in another, which she slid onto the table between them. Sitting in the booth with Teresa, Jennifer instantly recalled the camaraderie they had shared in elementary school. Teresa stared at Jennifer quizzically, narrowing her eyes as she lit up a cigarette and inhaled deeply, as if she were shielding her eyes from the smoke, which drifted upward. There but for the grace of some shrink go I, Jennifer thought to herself, looking at Teresa's lined face. One IQ test made a world of difference in our lives. Then she detested herself for feeling superior. Ironic, really, given that she had spent most of her years at St. Martin's envying Teresa. And now here she was, a graduate student who hadn't had a real job since she had been tossed scholarships for several years. She loved her life and she loved her fiancé, but what would she do if he — if her family — lost everything? Could she make her own path? Should she make some sacrifice to the gods to keep them from putting her to the test?

"So, what are you doing these days?" asked Jennifer.

"Mostly dodging bullets. I'm back in town to check up on Jason, my eldest. He's been avoiding his parole officer. Not very nice. So I guess I need to kick his ass." Teresa still had sinewy arms and flexed her biceps, which quivered visibly in her sleeveless tank top, a habit that Jennifer remembered from their youth and still admired. She distrusted women who got all their muscles at health clubs and only valued them as wardrobe accessories.

"I didn't know you had kids. Gee, I didn't even know you got married. Where are you living now, and what's your husband do?"

"Which one?" Teresa let out a deep cackle.

"Oh, I get it." Jennifer played with the sugar dispenser, flipping the opening flap up and down in a metallic rhythm. Why did she have to sound so prim and proper, just like her mother? It was Halloween in a few more days, and the jukebox on the wall had a cardboard ghost that jutted out its black tongue at them.

"There've been a couple, but they haven't stuck around. I have five kids, you know, but only one living with me right now. He's hell on wheels, but smart as a whip. At least one of them is turning out okay, I mean, I didn't blow it completely." Teresa ground out her cigarette, splaying the end of it. She still smoked Player's, just like she did in grade eight, and Jennifer couldn't imagine her without a cigarette in her hand. Teresa exhaled slowly and looked hard at Jennifer. Jennifer lowered her eyes. She shuffled her sandals under the table. The floor was gritty.

"Well, I guess I should push off and try to find the little bugger. Take care of yourself, eh?" Standing abruptly, Teresa placed a collection of loose change on the table. She swung her jean jacket around her shoulder by the index finger, brushed the cigarette package and lighter into her purse and strutted to the entrance. The waitress came to the table to take Jennifer's order. Both women stared after Teresa as she swung open the glass door and exited.

Jennifer felt guilty, silenced. She hadn't been able to tell Teresa about her life, though she would have liked to tell her about graduate school. And about her fiancé, who was her mother's candidate for the father of her grandchildren. About her plans to travel to South America as soon as her comprehensives were over. But she was out of her league here, especially since she had no kids, none of those battle stories that mothers love to swap. It felt unfair that Teresa shouldn't also be bragging about her travels and accomplishments. After all, they had both been the smartest girls back at St. Martin's. It took her back to the sense of unfairness that had plagued her throughout adolescence. Hard to believe that she and Teresa had once been so close, had sprouted their wings together. Smoked their first cigarettes together under the basketball hoop in the playground. And worst of all, Jennifer hadn't even been able to ask Teresa why she had run away from home all those years ago, why she hadn't bothered to stay in touch.

Jennifer too had run away, but in a different direction. It seems she had never stopped running since the summer that she scaled the ravine, that summer after grade eight when innocence ended. She'd lost her faith the same year she acquired her first serious boyfriend, a blond boy named Daryl. Before Daryl, there had been that horrible encounter in the woods with Gary Bennett, who was now a Famous Person. Over the years, Jennifer lost another kind of faith as Gary Bennett's harsh voice gradually faded from her memory. Just when she'd finally made his voice get out of her head, she had to hear it every time she turned on the damn local radio station. Now it was the golden voice of the star newscaster that rode the airwaves like some overearnest cowboy. The year that Gary had stolen something from her was the same year that she lost Teresa, and she still couldn't figure out why. Jennifer got herself back eventually, but what had happened to Teresa?

She let the waitress fill her coffee cup for the third time, although she didn't want any more, her brain already buzzing with caffeine. Sometimes she heard her own voice again these days, the one that's been silent all these years, the one that was there when Gary Bennett tried to drown it out one spring afternoon. Or a voice that whispers "NOW!" to Teresa as Jennifer accepts one more crumpled note from her desk. Sometimes she hears the voice of a nun giving instruction about the rules of mathematics. Or a voice that croons slow, sad Edith Piaf tunes. Voices from her past, still with her now. An older couple walked by the booth, hunching toward each other to talk across the noise of the tables full of boisterous young people. She felt a twinge of envy for the white-haired woman whose hand rested on the arm of the old man. While Jennifer ate alone.

She had stopped believing that IQ tests have anything to do with aptitude. She no longer believed in rules, knowing how easily they can be reversed to serve those who invent them. Nor was she certain exactly where the scars on her forearm had come from: her escape from the ravine, or that brutal floor hockey tournament. Both scars wrap around her wrist like ancient, gnarled trees, or like twin snakes.

GRADE EIGHT WAS THE YEAR HER FATE WAS SEALED. She was in grade eight when the proctor distributed the examination booklets to all the students in her home-room. It was a sunny day. She had just been out playing with several friends, and the dizzy panting that accompanied their games of hopscotch and double Dutch left her body still vibrating as she slid sideways into her desk. She was worrying about whether or not her mother would discover the theft of one of her coffee-coloured nylons. She'd dropped her red, white and blue India rubber ball inside the dark toe seam of the nylon. At lunch hour, after trading bologna sandwiches for ones with peanut butter and jam, Jennifer would play One, Two, Three O'Leary. This was a solo pursuit for, unlike the other girls, she did not take turns counting out loud with the player as the ball in the nylon whacked against the wall, waiting for a slip in the routine, a leg hit instead of the wall, or an escalating height against the wall that was unattainable. She did not share their glee in others' mistakes, and was afraid of her own. She would pin herself against the red brick wall of the school like the crucified Christ himself, and swing the weighted nylon above her head and arms, or between her raised legs, exhilarated at her own daring.

Jennifer's excitement over noon-hour pleasures was matched by her dread of Phys Ed, which was scheduled for the last period in the day. Although winter was over, the girls' floor hockey playoffs were not. Floor hockey was sheer torture for her. First there was the shame of the dressing room, where she would have to strip in front of the other girls and reveal the fact that she still wore an undershirt while all her girlfriends had their first Maidenform AA bras stretched across their chests. Girls with bras always took longer than normal to change into their gym clothes in the hope that everyone would notice that they too were among the initiated. She preferred a corner locker, where she undressed with her back turned to everyone. There was a ritual: she kept her kilt on until her gymsuit was pulled up underneath, and slid out of her blouse and quickly into the arms of the gymsuit. Unless of course you had something to show, this surreptitiousness was necessary. Then you pretended it was perfectly natural to stand there talking in your bra and undies indefinitely, flinging your arms open for emphasis, until you'd stretched out the conversation as long as possible.

Not only was she ashamed that she still wore an undershirt, but it was one of the types her grandmother sent from Europe, and it had lace trim with soft puckered folds stitched into the top. Her mother insisted she wear them because they were warm and sensible and because Jennifer had only begun to "sprout," as she put it; Jennifer looked in the bathroom mirror at her two tiny buds, thrusting her chest outward. Or her mother would say when Jennifer begged her to buy her a bra, "You are only starting to develop," as if it were a disease.

One day she'd seen Teresa changing in the middle of the room, her large breasts swinging from side to side. There were small red marks all around her neck and nipples. "What happened?" she asked innocently. "Hickeys," said Teresa proudly. It had taken Jennifer two days to admit to her friend that she didn't know what a hickey was. They were lying on her bed in her room, eating chips. "Here, give me your arm," said Teresa. She sucked on Jennifer's arm until it hurt. "That is a hickey," she said. For days after, Jennifer had thought that she'd been scarred for life. Gradually the ugly purple marks faded into small red dots. Jennifer had forgotten to ask what the purpose of them was, and then was too embarrassed to bring it up again. Teresa already rolled her eyes at Jennifer's ignorance far too often.

The hockey stars were two of the largest girls on the opposing team, Angelique Boutette and Mary MacArthur, and they'd had three years straight to fine-tune their techniques for eliminating any obstructions to their greater athletic glory. There was apparently nothing in the rules about the length of fingernails. Every night they filed their inch-long talons to sharp points that would spring out at other players like the switchblade one of the guys carried in his boot, leaving lifetime scars on anyone's arms who dared to cross their paths to the goal net. Jennifer had a permanent reminder of their viciousness in the form of a scar along her wrist. Sister Celine, the ancient nun who refereed the games, was brimming with energy and enthusiasm, but unfortunately her eyesight was failing.

Jennifer could have sworn that Angelique and Mary also filed their elbows at night, for invariably she'd be administered a painful jab in her newly sprouted buds whenever she tried to rescue the plastic ball from their control. This was one of the consequences of being short, of not shooting up early in adolescence like everyone else. Teresa said it was because she smoked too much and everyone knew that smoking stunted your growth. Once Jennifer had overheard one of the PTA mothers claim that girls are by nature less competitive than boys; obviously she had never met Angelique and Mary, whose towering frames were fuelled by an appetite for cheap starchy food and an equally voracious ambition to escape the neighbourhood boundaries. It was only Angelique who ever managed to get out, winning a basketball scholarship that took her as far away as the next diocese, where she accepted a job as a Phys Ed instructor, secured a marriage proposal, promptly gained one hundred and ten pounds, and quit her job to stay home and raise three children. Jennifer got the whole story from Anne Marie last year.

Jennifer compensated for not being an athletic beanpole by shrinking into her desk and hiding her face behind books. Although she was quiet by nature — indeed, she was often silent throughout an entire school day — still she could not avoid being noticed. Usually it was to be ridiculed as a browner, a brain, or for having the misfortune of being the only one in the class who had completed the Latin assignment the night before. Occasionally this affliction was transformed into an asset, when certain kids wanted help with their homework, and suddenly Jennifer was a star for ten whole minutes. Learning came easily to her; in fact, she was as frequently bored in the classroom as she was frightened in the schoolyard.

Sister Inez, the homeroom teacher, explained that every year Mount St. Joseph, the convent school located near the university, admitted one "needy" girl on full scholarship. Everyone groaned. Partly it was the stigma of being considered needy. But it was more that they all looked forward to finally escaping Catholic schools. Since none of their parents could afford the private Catholic high schools, they anticipated being released next year to attend the public high school where all the normal kids were also destined, equals at last. When the proctor, a mean boy with one elevated shoe whose weight he was not afraid to demonstrate, hobbled by Jennifer's desk with the examination booklet, her interest was piqued. The test had numerous puzzles and diagrams on the front page; it was an IQ test. Each question was a kind of jigsaw: which of these four words does not belong in the group? Which shape is different from the rest? There were math equations, and comprehension questions where she had to read a passage and deduce some conclusion.

Jennifer was watching Teresa out of the corner of her eye, seeing her doodle on the corners of the exam sheet. Jennifer could almost hear her thinking aloud, So who wants to go to some rich bitch school? She could feel the pull Teresa had on her, knew she wanted to make eye contact so that she could slip Jennifer the crumpled note she had in her fist. Teresa had this kind of mysterious hold on Jennifer. But Jennifer could already sense that they were pulling apart. For years they had rolled around under the lace canopy on Jennifer's bed, laughing so hard that she had thought she might pee her pants. When she listened to Teresa's dirty jokes, she felt wild, fearful, as if her dangerous new self was taking huge risks even being in the same bedroom where she practised being so good most nights when Teresa was not there. She was afraid her little sister Rita might smell how different the room was after Teresa left behind her scent of White Shoulders and Double Bubble. Teresa had signed her autograph book as "Your Best Friend Ever, T."

But then she read in Stacey's autograph book that Teresa had signed her name exactly the same way, and something changed. And Teresa started spending recess with the boys at the fence rather than going to the corner store with Jennifer. She tried not to act hurt as she clenched the cold quarters inside her mitten, jangling them in a futile attempt to get Teresa's attention.

It was later that same year that Teresa ran away from home, releasing Jennifer's mind from the certainties that were a daily diet. In running away, it was as if she let Jennifer forget all the platitudes that had made the majority of them, in their adult lives, prisoners to the pew and the office, sharing the same shades of Arborite countertops in their homes. Still, Jennifer missed her and wondered why it was that no one, not even the vociferous Gary Bennett, or the braggarts who claimed to have had her, spoke of her again except with a kind of incredulity that someone so familiar, so easy to target, could vanish from their lives so completely.

Throughout the test, Jennifer found herself staring at the fascinating books that were kept on the shelf in the cloakroom at the back of the classroom, above the radiator that hissed in winter as steam from soggy mittens gave the air the smell of burning wool. Sister Inez had her back turned to them and her face only half tilted toward the students. Jennifer could see the nun's profile sideways and watched her jowls jiggling up and down in her pleated wimple as she scrawled the notes on the chalkboard. All the students would dutifully copy the board work in notebooks as soon as the test was over. There was a good chance Jennifer could have accepted Teresa's note without any risk of interception, but she was reluctant. It was only partly related to the fact that the two of them had recently received a serious reprimand, when Jennifer had passed a note in math class that read, "Insert and multiply." This was a twisting of the math rule to "invert and multiply" when dividing fractions, a joke that she was surprised Sister Inez had even understood. Perhaps it had been Jennifer's crude drawing of an erect penis that had aided the nun's comprehension. After this, Jennifer became tired of explaining herself when everyone believed that she was a bad *influence* on Teresa. Teresa was trouble enough on her own, and needed no one to *influence* her.

It had a lot to do with Teresa's style, an intensity combined with an indifference to authority — exactly what the principal had warned about when describing to Jennifer's parents various bad *influences* on impressionable young girls. From where Jennifer sat, she could glimpse Teresa's restlessness as she fidgeted in her seat and watch her flutter her eyes in exasperation. Teresa was wearing baby blue eye shadow, a privilege her mother actually granted her. There was nothing forbidden at her house. Jennifer was envious. Like most of the other girls, Jennifer had to sneak out of the house early if she was wearing her mother's or her elder sister's makeup and make sure she wiped it off in the afternoon before shuffling home.

Teresa's father had a job at a downtown insurance firm and earned more money than most of the other fathers. Teresa said he was scary and wouldn't quit bugging her about everything, especially her marks at school. The family flaunted their wealth, said Jennifer's mother. She called them "profligate," which made no sense to Jennifer but sounded Biblical. Teresa had her own bedroom. The funny thing was that she said she envied Jennifer that she didn't have to sleep alone. Teresa's house was larger and filled with modern furniture that quickly lost its fashionable patina as numerous Catholic offspring jumped on the brocade sofas, or spilled orangeade on the matching La-Z-Boy. Teresa's mother had a permanent suntan because she went to Florida every winter with her husband, leaving Teresa's Aunt Mary — "a roaring drunk," Teresa called her — in charge of the kids. Back home in the summer, she would sprawl elegantly in her bikini on the chaise lounge in the backyard, smoking cigarettes, painting her nails and drinking something fizzy with lots of ice cubes and limes floating in it, holding her sunglasses up briefly to say, "How was school, girls?" Before they could answer, she'd blurt out, "Now you kids just help yourself to whatever you want in the kitchen." And there were always snacks in the kitchen: the store-bought kind that you saw advertised on TV, the kind that most of their parents could never afford. Twinkies by the dozen box. Giant packages of Oreos. Raisin bread. Bags of Hostess chips in boxes.

It was a kind of paradise few of the other kids could even imagine. Teresa and two of her sisters also wore braces, an unheard-of luxury. Although they called her "Tinsel Teeth," everyone knew the braces gave her special status. She still ate junk food even though she claimed her orthodontist — how she drawled out the pronunciation of that word — had forbidden it. Teresa's mother never cared if she came home for dinner on time, or nagged her about ruining her appetite or brushing her teeth, braces or not. No one made her take piano lessons. Her mother didn't even seem to mind that she'd failed grade seven twice, although her father was always complaining about her grades. Teresa was luckier than any of them.

Jennifer's mother had no kind words for Teresa, or her family. "If I were as rich as that woman," she said, referring to Teresa's mother, "I 'd have lots of projects. I could get on with my sewing, for example. I don't think she even keeps an eye on those kids, just throws money at them whenever they need her attention." Jennifer often wished to avoid her mother's attention, which was far too vigilant and critical.

She kept her distance. Out of fear, out of envy, she held back from declaring Teresa as her best friend, in the way that girls did, changing their minds every few weeks. She would hesitate ever so slightly when Teresa assumed she would help her with her homework. Teresa had no such reservations about Jennifer, and was determined to educate her, which she set about with missionary zeal. She swore with finesse. She taught Jennifer how to blow smoke rings and how to kiss with tongues. Gary Bennett watched them do the latter, peering around the corner of the school building, his eyes wide with disbelief. Teresa noticed him spying on them, and she taunted Jennifer mercilessly for nearly two weeks in her singsong voice, the same one she used for skipping rhymes: "Gary's got a hard-on for Je-en-ny," or "I'm gonna te-ell, Jenny's in lu-uve," or "Gary's got a cru-ush on Jen-ee-ee-ee."

That was the thing about Teresa: you couldn't be certain where her allegiances lay. She did not insist that Jennifer vow, for instance, "Cross your heart and hope to die," as all the other girls did, because she never needed to share her secrets with anyone, never required conspiracies or bargains or promises. Whenever she played hide and seek or frozen tag, she would announce in her loud braying voice, "fifteen and counting," but there was no guarantee she'd actually turned her back while everyone else sought hiding places.

Often at recess Teresa could be seen standing at the chain-link fence, talking with the Protestants, whose schoolyard bordered theirs. She always had candy from the Red and White store that was at the mall in the lot across from the two schools, usually stolen and therefore more delicious, even though it was well known that students weren't supposed to go off the property at recess. She would generously pour granular mounds of purple Kool-Aid powder from brightly coloured striped straws into outstretched palms, or blow large bubbles with her Double Bubble gum, which never stuck in her braces. This was one reason why Jennifer believed Teresa was blessed with unique powers.

One day Jennifer saw Teresa talking by the fence with a boy whose upper lips looked like the suede of a peach skin. Brian was very tall. He was supposed to have failed grade six twice. Rumour had it that she had gone all the way with him, whereas most of the girls had never passed first base with any boy. She had a precocious air about her and was certainly, as Jennifer's mother would have described it, more developed than any of the other girls. All the cute boys, Christians on both sides of the fence, said disgusting things to her that any other girl would have been taught to pretend not to have heard. "Come and get your T-bone," they taunted her.

"So what exactly do you do with them when you meet those guys after school?" Jennifer asked her, wanting all the gory details.

"I only let them cop a feel when I want to," she said. "I'm very fussy. Brian says he's crazy about my tits. He loves to stick his nose between them. He says I'm special, that Catholic girls do it best. God, you'd think I was the fucking Virgin Mary, the ways he goes on about it!" At this she tilted her head back and roared with laughter. Jennifer felt stupid, having no stories of her own to compare.

One day, just before the bell rang, Jennifer overheard an exchange at the fence between Teresa and Brian. She had seen him with Teresa at the drugstore downtown once when Jennifer was out shopping with her mother. There were several others milling about. Although they'd been taught to regard such guys as misguided because they were Protestant and were all going to hell anyway, secretly they admired them, not the least of all because their uniforms were better than the Catholic ones. Instead of navy plaid kilts, the girls wore forest green tunics with school crests sewn on the yokes and the boys had grey flannel short trousers with cuffs that made them appear more distinguished than the bony-kneed Catholic boys in their navy serge shorts.

Brian didn't even wait for the rest of the kids to leave the fence.

"You slut," he spat on the ground at Teresa's feet. Their bell rang about one minute before the Protestant bell did — another punishment for being Catholic, for being on the wrong side of the fence. Jennifer could remember Teresa making her pronouncement to him in a cool and haughty voice that in no way betrayed any panic.

"You'd better pray I get to bleed very soon." She turned her back on white-faced Brian and strode away from him at the exact moment that her bell rang. Teresa had an exquisite sense of timing.

This sense of timing operated even in church. When she went to get communion at mass she managed to capture everyone's attention. Gary Bennett, who was serving as an altar boy, could not take his eyes off Teresa — or at least, off her chest — his fists grasping the mitre in the procession as clawlike as those of the Damned in the scary picture Jennifer had seen in *The Illustrated Dante*. Stealing a sideways glance at Teresa, Gary nearly tripped in his floor-length carmine-red cassock with its mandarin collar and fancy covered buttons from collar to hem. On top of the cassock he wore a lamb-white, mid-calf surplice, complete with lace trim at the cuffs and hem. How could a boy who looked like a rough beast at recess could be transformed into such a cherubic vision of saintliness once a week? Maybe that was what Father Sebastian meant by the mystery of transubstantiation.

Jennifer turned up the corners of the gold-edged pages in her missal with her white net-gloved fingers, and stared at the lurid colours of the statues in their niches. She tried to determine which of her new Laurentian coloured pencils would match the graphic red that dripped from the open, stretched palms of our Lord. Sometimes she studied all the holy cards she'd been collecting from various relatives and tried to decide which one was her current favourite. Her family sat in one of the closer pews — choice seats because sitting there meant that one could watch each communicant pass by and slowly glide up to the altar railing, solemn and majestic as brides, showing off the latest fashions. Of course Jennifer was supposed to be looking pious and contemplating with awe the body of Christ as it melted in her mouth. But out of one corner of her eye she was really watching what each of her girlfriends was wearing, full of remorse that she herself had been seen in the same outfit for two Sundays in a row now. Jennifer wore her cousin's hand-me-down wool dress, whose plainness her mother had tried to improve by fastening a lace dickey to the collar and detachable lace cuffs to the sleeves. At home they had seemed magnificent, even vaguely Victorian, as Jennifer had admired their effect in the full-length mirror. Now she merely felt tawdry as she observed all the newest styles from the Eaton's catalogue on each girl who self-consciously moved away from the priest after he had placed the host in their mouths. She could tell they knew they were parading for the whole congregation as they changed course and walked along the first pew, treating their one minute of glory as if it were a stroll down a catwalk. Jennifer was usually near the end of the communion line, and so had the rapt attention of the entire seated congregation, leaning on its knees. She never failed to feel embarrassed, felt the shame rising up her neck and turning her face red while her heart pounded and the heat from her wool dress itched along the backs of her legs.

When she came home from church, Jennifer felt the weight of Sunday afternoon descend upon her. Her mother would do her best to distract her when the family returned home from mass, baking trays of chocolate chip cookies while observing her Sunday ritual of listening to Edith Piaf croon on the hi-fi. If this were the week Jennifer's father got paid, they would have slices of kielbasa from the Polish corner store, served on Ritz crackers, to tide them over until dinner. She didn't care that her mother looked morose when she refused these treats, complaining that they gave her pimples. She wanted to punish somebody.

"Why are you always trying to feed me? Haven't you got anything better to do than to think about people's stomachs all day?" When Jennifer's mother said nothing, she'd feel wretched and reach over to give her mother a hug.

"Don't touch my hair. I just got it done." Jennifer thought it was impossible to disturb her mother's stiff and lacquered beehive, but said nothing. Her mother was serious about music, wanted Jennifer to excel at classical music, though she herself was fonder of Harry Belafonte, Tom Jones, Frank Sinatra, and of course Edith Piaf. Jennifer never made it past Royal Conservatory grade five, and her mother never let her forget her disappointment. The best part about going to Teresa's house was that there was no piano there, no one to ask her to play something for them. Jennifer had loved being outside too much, even as a child, and her hours of music practice were a misery when she longed to be swimming or running around. As Sunday afternoon wore on, following the fading of "Je ne regrette rien," Jennifer had to practise piano right after her sister had finished and pushed the bench back in. The bench seat was still warm as she played "Für Elise" over and over, imagining some romantic Stranger listening beyond the door in sincere admiration. Her mother proudly believed that she was genuinely interested in perfecting the piece. Jennifer had other ideas: the newspaper boy, a gorgeous hunk who lived a mere three blocks away, was due to collect his money every Sunday afternoon at about this time. Jennifer envisioned him standing outside the door,

moved by the tune upon which he had accidentally eaves-
dropped, curious to know how long she'd been playing,
impressed by her musical sensitivity, begging for more.
And so she played the same piece repeatedly, losing herself
in a spiral of reverie. Not because the music moved her,
but because her fantasy could take her places, out of doors
and beyond the pale gold matching sofa and chairs that
filled the room. Eventually even her mother suggested that
perhaps Jennifer had practised enough for the day. She
always felt exhausted after these Sunday afternoons at the
piano. She can still hear her mother's voice as she leaned
over to interrupt Jennifer's reverie.

"It's time for a little quiet now," entreated her mother.
"I need to get my novena said before making dinner."
Sunday dinner was the centrepiece of her week.

It was over a Sunday dinner that Jennifer's parents
announced she would be going to the convent the
following year. The day of that examination had changed
everything. Jennifer had won the scholarship to the
convent, with the proviso that her behaviour must
improve; obviously the principal had been consulted about
her suitability as the annual convent charity case. It was
implied that an outward increase in piety would also be
considered in Jennifer's favour. She ignored such recom-
mendations, knowing that as long as she maintained high
grades, she was set for tuition and board for all of high
school. She swelled with pride, even though many of her
classmates regarded her with pity and disdain.

During the week that Jennifer's convent fate was sealed, Gary Bennett was promoted to lay reader at church. His voice, always loud and boisterous, had deepened dramatically in the past year. The parish priest was eager to point out Gary to other of his "young men" who, if not of the same size or maturity, were the same age as Gary and likewise keen to demonstrate their commitment to the Church. He often referred students to the parable of the ten talents. Jennifer never knew until many years later that "talents" referred to coins rather than any God-given aptitude. Later in his adult life, Gary's booming voice would continue to be chained to public service as he advanced through radio announcer jobs, beginning locally as a commentator at county fairs and sporting events, and as a DJ at graduation parties. His voice could be heard everywhere, with its gradual crescendo of importance and authority. When he was twenty-two, he married a plain, shy girl and produced four boys. By his late twenties, Gary had become a recognized voice on the CBC. People at church spoke proudly of him. He was getting ahead, they said.

At St. Martin's, every one of them wanted to get ahead, to move away from the chain-link fence that kept them corralled during recess in winter. Sometimes their tongues froze to the metal and became so stuck they had to rip them off. Jennifer had won her escape from that schoolyard and rejoiced that the upcoming year at the convent was bound to bring the poise and sophistication to her life that everyone dreamed of. But she still had another two months to survive at St. Martin's. And she never envisioned Teresa not being there to share the final moments of boredom with her. Nor that Teresa wouldn't do just as well as Jennifer once she escaped.

There was no note, no surreptitious phone call, no warning. Teresa simply left town. No one knew why. Jennifer was stunned. Between the fenced yard of the school and the newly developed suburb where she lived was a ravine, a wild forested no-man's-land that the developers had not yet pillaged because its steeply slanting and unpredictable terrain made it uneconomical for building houses, at least at present. The ravine was the locale for all their ghost stories, their exaggerated tales of disappeared children who exposed themselves to strangers. Some of her classmates speculated that they would find Teresa's bones down there one day, that all the McDonald's wrappers and empty foil Humpty Dumpty bags were clear evidence that some pervert lived down there year-round, and she had been giving it to him for free. Without Teresa around, Jennifer became increasingly self-sufficient, dreamy, a loner who imagined there was no necessity in acquiring new friends since she would be moving on anyway. Finally she understood that her school life was to be lived out in what Father Sebastian called "limbo," during which she felt she was neither a kid nor a real grown-up high school student. Her mother complained constantly that daydreaming would get Jennifer nowhere.

THERE WERE TRAILS LEADING DOWN INTO THE ravine, only one of which was used regularly in winter as a toboggan slide that they slid down on a plastic flying saucer, or, when her parents wouldn't buy her another one of those, a garbage can lid. This was the path Jennifer sometimes took home when there was enough daylight. There was a hole at the corner of the school's chain-link fence where it was ripped away from the pole and Jennifer could just squeeze through it, run quickly down the ravine trail and up the other side of the hill. She would emerge between the yards of two of the newer homes whose owners, with any luck, were at work during the day. If not, Jennifer had learned to bow her head meekly and say, "Yes, ma'am, I won't do it again." A small price to pay for saving at least twenty minutes by not taking the long way home. And in the advancing light of spring, any additional time to play between school and supper was precious.

It must still have been spring. The trilliums were just coming out on the floor of the ravine. They had all been taught not to pick them because they were the provincial flower and there was a fine for getting caught. Jennifer was trying to remember the amount of the fine, weighing whether or not it was worth the risk to pluck one of those lovely white blossoms as it gleamed in the strong filtered sunlight, where dappled shadows gave it a variegated appearance. She didn't hear the crunch of footsteps on stale winter leaves. She thought of running, but then saw the hockey jacket and realized it was just Gary Bennett. She had noticed him staring at her at choir practice. Jennifer let him catch up and started talking to him, but recognized something not quite right about his face. He seemed agitated, speaking much more quickly than he did when she talked to him in the hallways. Before this unsettling thought had rooted itself in her mind, she realized he had both hands on her shoulders and was pushing her onto the ground. Jennifer's books fell out of the plastic milk bag she had been carrying them in, and her treasured Laurentian pencils lay scattered all around her.

His voice was deep and strong like a man's as he fumbled with the buttons on her blouse.

"Stupid cunt," he muttered. "You thought that by hiding behind Teresa no one would notice what a cock tease you are?" Jennifer was more shocked by that word, by the injustice of it being applied to her, than she was by the probing of his fingers. Gary's voice grew louder and more commanding. "Get over here now, Jennifer, if you know what's good for you." Her own voice seemed dim and inaccessible. This was nothing like the slow seduction she had fantasized about when she pictured the moment of losing her virginity, imagining she would be redeemed by an ideal lover whose face resembled an older version of the newspaper boy. Not the large, pimpled face of Gary Bennett. More in disappointment than outrage, Jennifer spat in his face. She scratched at his neck, and jumped up when he turned his face away. Then she felt her fury building. She kicked out at him, aiming between his legs, but her foot made no contact.

"Stupid bitch. You should be grateful I picked you. You have the flattest chest in the world." He lunged toward her again.

Jennifer broke into a run. She ran up the bank of the ravine, scraping her knees and arms as maple twigs pierced her skin. She panted all the way to the cul-de-sac where the two new houses backed onto the ravine, for once wishing that someone would come out to scold her for trespassing. As she climbed the metal fence, Jennifer ripped open her arm from elbow to forearm, leaving pieces of her skin on top of the jagged metal twists on top of the chain-link fence. Not until she smelled the black tar of the asphalt baking in the strong spring sun did she look back, but Gary wasn't following her. She'd caught a glimpse of his mottled face as she had risen from the ground. It was transfixed with a stupid stare, an intense inward focused look that made him appear cross-eyed. Later Jennifer made her big sister Mary accompany her back to retrieve her books and pencils; she lied and told Mary she had put them down when playing hide and seek. Jennifer told her mother she'd been climbing the school fence when her bare arm had caught.

"Great," said her mother sarcastically. "Now you'll have a scar to match the one on the inside of your arm. The one you got from that floor hockey stick. You'll have to wear long sleeves the rest of your life. Two scars on one arm, just imagine! No sleeveless gowns for you, young lady. Never mind, you don't want to turn into a hussy like your friend Teresa. Imagine her going and getting knocked up before she even finished grade school. And her parents getting divorced now. I never did like that father of hers, that look in his eye."

"What do you know?" screamed Jennifer. "Nobody knows anything about Teresa. You just shut up about her!"

BUT NOW HER COFFEE WAS COLD AND BITTER and she was never going to have time to get to the bank machine if she didn't want to be late getting back to work. She still had so many unanswered questions about Teresa. About whether it was really Brian who got her pregnant. There were so many possibilities. In spite of her mother's predictions, Jennifer had worn sleeveless gowns, and patiently answered questions about her scars. She thought they conferred a certain mystery. At least they gave her a sense of history, she thought now, glancing over the bill for her coffee and sandwich. She rose slowly and pulled on her trench coat. It was getting chilly. The waitress smiled at her and nodded her head in the direction of the cash register. A few minutes later she met her there and handed Jennifer back her change without looking at her. Jennifer left through the same door that Teresa had closed only minutes earlier.

Ghost

But though my wing is closely bound
My heart's at liberty;
My prison walls cannot control
The flight, the freedom of the soul.
— *Jean Guyon (1648 – 1717), "A Prisoner's Song,"*
Castle of Vincennes, France

FRIDAY NIGHTS ARE USUALLY THE WORST, THINKS Kathryn. She keeps herself busy in all sorts of ways, and talks to herself. But it doesn't help. Listening to her co-workers discuss family outings for the upcoming weekend makes her feel lonely, small. Even their complaints about the heavy traffic jams when they are leaving town fill her with envy. Were Friday nights worse before her marriage broke up? She asks herself this as she tears apart another piece of pizza, mildly repulsed by the stale cardboard smell. Pizza has been her traditional treat on Fridays, her consolation prize, a comfort food connected with misery for longer than Kathryn cares to remember. She is not as blue tonight as she has been on previous Friday nights; something has shifted. She has stopped having the hallucinations that troubled her, sent her scurrying to the optometrist, who told her that her vision had changed, that she was growing older. Not what she wanted to hear.

It wasn't that Jeff had been a bad man. He had a good appetite. He had made money — more when it suited him, less when he was uninspired. He made lots of noise about how hard he was working. Kathryn recalls their days of romance. Jeff had, for instance, proposed to her at Stratford while they were having a picnic of paté, crackers and Merlot by the riverbank, in between *Hamlet* and *A Midsummer Night's Dream*. Both of them had been a bit lightheaded. Coming out of the theatre, the ghost of Hamlet's father stayed imprinted on Kathryn's retina. She blinked in the sunlight as they settled beside the river.

"Did you know that swans mate for life?" he had said, watching the long-necked birds glide gracefully across the water. Their wings were folded back in upon their smooth white bodies, and Kathryn knew that they were mute swans, not trumpeters. She remembered reading somewhere that the down-covered cygnets could walk and swim a few hours after hatching. She had assumed that he was implying that this lifetime habit of mating was desirable for human beings too. Taken it so much for granted that she had failed to ask him what he meant by it. Of that moment, Kathryn recalled only the warmth of his eyes.

She thinks back now to previous Friday nights filled with longing, sleepless nights when she felt like howling at the moon, "Why aren't you here?" Full-moon light pouring through the venetian blinds. She remembers another full-moon night, during the first year that they met, when he brought her incense and washed her with a new lavender soap. Wasn't Jeff influenced by the same moon? Didn't its rays penetrate his window at night? On those nights it was her husband's absence she was mentally haranguing him for; it was her anguished protest, uttered only to herself and only hours after their typical Friday night phone calls. Her fury at his distant and preoccupied voice. Her yearning was so great when he was away. Yet she could never fault him for not being dutiful in his calls, and of course it was the nature of his work as a pharmaceutical salesman that kept him away from home most of the time.

Jeff appeared to be hardworking and dedicated, really. If she were to measure that by how much time he spent away. He was determined to retire before fifty-five, he had claimed. Kathryn admired his intelligence, but she couldn't understand why he didn't want to be at home with the kids more often. One night he announced that her demands on him to be more available were unreasonable.

"You knew what kind of work I was in when you met me. You knew I'd be away a lot. So how can you expect me to focus on the home front when I'm busy trying to meet my sales quota? And why do you always whine about how tired you are whenever I call? Don't you think I'm tired too? Maybe if you had adopted a positive attitude from the beginning, we wouldn't be like this." In response, she had kicked the back door screen in, her sandals denting the wire mesh, and shouted at him, even though she already knew that there was no way out. She no longer remembered what she had said, only that it was full of expletives.

"You should learn to control your aggression," Jeff had responded in a calm voice, and quoted his favourite passage from the *Tao Te Ching*: "The highest good is like water. Water gives life to the ten thousand things and does not strive." He had once lectured her on the ability of water to wear rock down. If she were a rock, she would have hurled herself at him that night. Instead she had tried to breathe deeply as she pulled the roast out of the oven. There were ten thousand things that she had wanted to say.

"Gabe, I want you to set the table. And Nathan, empty the dishwasher so we have enough glasses for everyone," she said, trying to sound calm. She rearranged the flowers, moving them from the centre to the edge of the glass table in the dining room, and set down a plate of cold pickles and radishes where the water ring from the flower vase had been. Jeff had sat in one of the chairs, the newspaper spread out before him, looking distracted when she rumpled the newspaper to make him lift his elbows so she could spread out the placemats. Jeff always liked to sit at the head of the table, a place Nathan normally occupied when his father was absent. It was understood that Kathryn would stay in the chair closest to the kitchen door, since she always served everyone, scurrying back and forth to the kitchen, the last one to sit down. She had tried switching seats with one of the kids when Jeff was away, schooling herself to tell them to fetch their own glasses of milk or whatever they needed, but found herself automatically resorting to her old place whenever Jeff returned.

"How long are you home for this time, Dad?" Nathan had asked. "Can you come watch our playoff game on Monday?" He was banging the glasses down on the table so loudly that Kathryn was afraid they might shatter.

"I don't know yet. We'll have to see," replied Jeff, not looking up from the paper. He was still handsome, thought Kathryn then. Even though greying at the temples.

"What do you think of Mommy's new dress?" Gabe interjected. "I helped her pick out the colour when we were at the mall. Maybe I'll get to wear it too, if she'll let me."

This time he had raised his head slowly, then returned his gaze to the newspaper as he turned the page. His grey eyes were transparent, like a guppy's, so that it was hard for her to look at them most of the time.

"I'm sure it will look great on your mother, once she loses a couple more pounds." Kathryn had felt rage building in her chest, but said nothing. He's just stressed out from being away so long, doesn't mean to be insensitive, she kept saying to herself like a mantra, but it hadn't calmed her down at all.

"Nathan got straight A's on his report card," she interjected, trying to focus on the children. Her wrist trembled as she sliced bread.

"That's nice, Nathan," Jeff said, patting his son on the head. Nathan scraped his chair under the table, dragging it behind him as he pulled up to the table. He was already reaching out for his second pickle on the condiment plate. Nathan's head lifted from his plate, and he chewed and swallowed his food quickly, then opened his mouth to speak. Jeff had been staring straight ahead and did not notice him.

"Did I tell you about the man who was staying in the hotel room beside me, who came running down the hall in his underwear to tell me it looked as if there was a fire in my room and smoke was coming out under the door? He was obviously drunk or hallucinating, since there wasn't smoke for miles." Jeff turned expectantly to Gabe, who laughed on cue. As the whole family usually did. Kathryn and the children had listened to more of his stories about funny customers and strange hotels. She would be grateful when he left again, she had thought. She was always grateful for the return to their routine. How grateful would she really be if he were home more often?

When the phone rang the next time he was away, she picked it up and hoped he would hear from her tone of voice that she was exhausted. And that she could not wait to see him again.

"I'll be so grateful when you get back tomorrow and can give me a break from the kids," she had said.

"Actually, I won't be home tomorrow after all. I'm working an extra week so I can take time off next month. It'll be more money for us."

In the background, she could hear the shouts of people greeting one another in whatever bar he was calling from, could hear the clink of glasses and the shrill, drunken laughter of patrons arriving or leaving.

"But it's not fair," she protested. She realized she was whining like one of the children when they were younger, but could not help herself.

"I'm doing it for us, honey," he said, as he always said, his distraction and fatigue evident in his clipped sentences. Later she lay in bed, full of self-recriminations for having spoken of her need of him, for not consistently maintaining her usual brisk and confident tone while on the phone with him. She had been selfish, and did not think of how selfless he could be in working so hard for all of them.

"But you're a strong woman, you can handle it. I know you can," he'd tried to soothe her, and his words had echoed in her mind. The upturn in his voice signalled that he was wrapping up their conversation with the usual morale-boosting phrases. And what woman doesn't want to hear that she is strong? Would she protest — no, I am weak, dependent and needy? So instead Kathryn tossed in bed, trying again to convince herself that these long absences were romantic, that they kept love alive — the same tired clichés she had chanted to herself over the years, but they were wearing thin. Over the next week, she moved through her days telling herself that all the tea towels and pillowcases on the clothesline were bleaching white, that watching them flap in the wind satisfied her, gave her pleasure in a world that was orderly and clean, pleasure enough until his return.

One morning in her office, the air conditioning had broken down, and she had come home to the children's demands for a picnic dinner, her patience ready to snap. Kathryn had been seeking refuge in the coolness of the basement, hauling laundry out of the washing machine to bring outside to hang up on the clothesline, when Jeff had returned home after being away for five weeks. She had sent the children to play next door, so no one had heard him walk through the front door after quietly turning his key in the lock, nor had anyone heard him when he moved through the house in search of Kathryn before heading out into the garden. When she finally noticed him as she whipped the wet clothes flat to hang on the line, she heard before she saw that he was plucking weeds.

"Jeff!" she had cried in surprise. Her mind already leapt ahead to the new silk shirt she would put on for him later that evening, the luxury foods she could add to their outdoor picnic. She had waited for him to move toward her, anticipating his kiss.

"You haven't kept up the garden, I see."

Kathryn had felt her heart being lost in the heat that expanded in waves of late afternoon humidity between them as she stood on the deck and watched him pull more weeds. What the hell did he know about working full-time and caring for kids full-time, never having a moment to yourself? About driving to Little League games, swimming lessons and parent-teacher meetings? About neighbourhood organizing committees? There was a huge gulf between them, a space between the raised garden beds that was unbridgeable, that she could not traverse even if she willed herself to step forward. She knew that she should reach across that expanse anyway, mutter endearments and claim her embraces from him. But too often lately she had come to the conclusion that these were no longer hers for certain, these familiar gestures of affection. Kathryn had looked through a watery mirage created by the heat at the bent figure of her husband wearing his khaki shorts and hiking boots. All that she could summon then, after all those years of marriage, was lust and pity. She could not have moved. She felt her spine stiffen, felt as though she were a figure in a still life, aging into a frozen tableau. Something in her knew then that the moment was irreversible, that life with Jeff would never be the same again.

"If you pull the weeds, just a few every day, then they wouldn't take over like this. I've told you over and over."

JEFF HAD ALSO REPEATED ANOTHER OF HIS FAVOURITE phrases when he left her and the children: "I'm doing it for us, honey."

He had spoken of the need for each of them to pursue their own karma, hoped for her that she would one day discover her soul mate too, claimed that she was being granted freedom. What his own karma was he had been less specific about.

She was used to seeing the back of him as he went out the door. Relieved, often. So when Kathryn's husband left for good, she had not expected to feel his absence in such a physical way, her entire body flooded with instinct. At first she would raise her hands to her face and be able to distinguish his scent on her palms. Astonished at the naked and automatic faith of her body as it performed its daily rituals, touching, cleaning, she remembered the touch of his flesh, her fingers retaining the measure of his hands, the dimensions of his wrists and the shape of each of his fingers. She recalled the deep smooth mocha cave of his mouth after coffee in the mornings.

She felt entitled to missing his weight in bed and had anticipated the long ache that ran from her ankles along the insides of her thighs. But she found compensation in the coolness of clean sheets, the joy of stretching her limbs across the queen-sized bed that was now entirely hers, a starfish encountering a wide ocean of rippled cotton. Odd that that had been the first ritual she had performed the night Jeff had removed the last cardboard box and walked down the driveway: Kathryn changed the linen on her bed and all the towels in the bathroom with a frenetic energy that astonished her. This was a weekly ritual, but not cleaning house. Lately, sensing that something unusual was coming into her life, she had stopped cleaning the house. Recently she had postponed any housecleaning until dust bunnies under the bed rolled themselves into boulders. But that night she had done three loads of laundry and, still unable to sleep, had rearranged the furniture in her bedroom. Jeff had never liked the bed under the window; he'd complained of the light disturbing him in the mornings. Kathryn delighted in being a morning person and, being contrary, as he would have said, she was equally delighted to stay up for most of that first night after his final departure, finally lying down at four in the morning. She felt a little thrill, knowing that the sun would soon pour through the slats in the venetian blinds and wake her in only two hours, throwing its striped patterns across her skin.

At three in the morning, she'd found herself cleaning kitchen cupboards and switching the glassware from the china cabinet to the shelf above the sink, congratulating herself on this step-saving change. She dragged furniture across the living room floor, and could hear Jeff's voice in the back of her mind — further back, this time — "Watch it! You're scratching the damn floors again!" By the time Kathryn was peeling back the wallpaper in the bathroom, all she could hear was the faint trilling of an early morning robin. Again she fell into bed, exhausted but strangely exhilarated.

The next month continued with the same euphoric shifts. Kathryn told herself that Jeff was dead. It made it easier than thinking he had really left them. But then she remembered how she had felt when her mother died: it seemed that her relation to the dead continued to change because she continued to love them. She wondered if she stayed in his memory, or if she even wanted to be fixed there. What remains when love has gone? What comes, what goes?

At night sometimes, Kathryn found herself listening for the fall of footsteps in the hallway that would have announced Jeff's arrival, the way she used to at the beginning of their marriage. He was not really gone, she convinced herself, had not abandoned her and the children. It must have been an accident, his death. In the mirror in the mornings she was certain she saw the shadow of his face, the clarity of his eyes. She was filled with the memory of their first meeting, the sudden visceral expansion, the shifting of molecules as her heart opened, her mind changed, the universe altered and room was created for something new. The liquidity of memory, the lucidity of the moment, as the boundaries of what she found erotic were stretched outward. It was that memory of love, the illusion that it could be restored or reciprocated, that she continued to miss in Jeff.

He had taken the vacuum cleaner, strangely committed to its ownership after berating Kathryn for getting sucked into the slick promises of a Filter Queen salesman. When she had paid for it, in installments, over the past five years, he had chastised her for needing to always have the best, mocked her for being too "house proud." She tried to imagine him dragging it around a room, when she had never even seen him turn it on. Now she pushed away the larger pieces of lint from the carpet with a broom, and was not bothered by what remained. Who needs a bloody vacuum cleaner, anyway? The disorientation in her kitchen, into which she stumbled at odd hours, inspired Kathryn. She shifted her mealtimes, began sleeping less and experienced an appetite for cucumbers at breakfast that she indulged without judgement. For over a week, she ate raw onion sandwiches at supper: thick slabs of Spanish onion on buttered rye that left her eyes watering and made her grateful that Jeff was not there to comment sarcastically on her breath or draw back, repulsed by her kisses. She tasted onion for the first time, and could not get enough. She drank tea instead of coffee; left her bed unmade, and did not look for herself in the shadows. Her energy was boundless, and she lost the ten pounds she had been battling all winter, this time without effort. Adrenalin kept her running through the days and the nights. Nathan and Gabe told her she looked fantastic.

⤙

SO WHEN, TWO AND A HALF MONTHS LATER, GRIEF welled up inside her throat and Kathryn could not swallow without a heavy stone constricting the flow of her breath, she was stunned. It was late in the afternoon, shortly before she had to go and pick up the kids. Kathryn was standing at the kitchen window that overlooked the garden when the apparition approached from the pile of rubble that Jeff had claimed he would one day transform into a Japanese rock garden. The ghost was like Jeff in appearance, and the sight of his straining calf muscles below his shorts as he bent to pull weeds from the garden took Kathryn's breath completely away. Of all gestures to miss in a person, of all parts of Jeff's body over which she had rhapsodized for hours, stroked into her memory, this one would not have been the highlight. Are these the things she will miss? When she could barely recall his kiss?

She watched him bend over again, noting once more the taut sinuousness of his calf muscle, and marvelled at the lust she felt quivering through her legs. He seemed transformed into the younger man he had been when they had first met, his eyes full of hope. Not the over-weight, middle-aged and balding man who had left her late one night. Slowly she opened the porch door, and slipped down the stairs toward the patio, afraid to disturb the ghost of Jeff. But nothing seemed to affect him. It was then she understood: Jeff was impervious, and would be spared everything. Some other woman would pick up the new Jeff, dust him off and he would continue in his next life without the inconveniences of grief or memory. As the apparition stood up to stretch, Kathryn admired his expressionless face, and the brief glimpse she had of the nape of his neck when he rolled back the collar of his shirt. Tentatively she reached out and touched him there, and ran her finger along the curve of his spine. Slowly, as if unable to comprehend her presence, he turned his distracted face toward her, blinking to avoid the sun. Kathryn grew bolder, reached both her arms around, recalling the set of his shoulders and the shape of his hands as she pulled them around her waist.

But there was something different about this ghost: he responded to her touch, and she felt his heart beating beneath the plaid flannel shirt, an echo of her own rhythm. His face brightened, and suddenly he whirled her around, lifting her from the garden bed and spinning her in a waltz toward the pear tree. She felt her body yielding to him, melting, in spite of her mind's protest. Surprised by her ardour, she turned to whisper to him, and he whispered something back so gently that it was unintelligible. "Again," she entreated, but he was gone; she held her arms in the air in a mock ritual dance.

Running home from work, Kathryn encountered the ghost late every afternoon in the garden, and continued

to dance with him. Some routines are harder than others
to abandon, she decided. Unlike Jeff, he did not trip her,
and danced well, without any awkwardness. She dreamed
at night of seducing him, and it was always perfect.
Floating through her work in the mornings, she raced
home to swing the back gate open, uncertain whether she
would find him tilling the soil as usual, and relieved and
grateful to see that he had not changed, that he beckoned
toward her eagerly each time. In this apparition she
sensed the potential for permanent, unconditional love.
As summer unfolded, Kathryn realized she was in love
with the phantom; lust ran in her veins like sap and she
felt open, receptive, in love with all the people she met,
all the objects she picked up. Every man she met had
some gesture that reminded her of him; she saw something of him in everyone and she was enamoured with
total strangers. When she recalled Jeff's complaint that
she was shallow, uptight and had no feelings, she realized that he had not known what she was really like, had
never come toward her with the gentleness of this
apparition. The ghost was mute, and his gestures were
beckoning, not coercive. She ached for him with tenderness and a burning sense of loss.

And then, just as suddenly as the ghost had appeared
in her life, he was gone. It took weeks before Kathryn
could tolerate such total absence. She wanted to remain
with him, to indulge in their comforting rituals. One
evening, smelling the jasmine at dusk, Kathryn realized

that her yearning was mistaken: that to remain with someone dead was to abandon not just him, but also herself. All these months, when Kathryn felt Jeff's ghost entreating her, filling her with loneliness, she had been mistaken. She had misunderstood his signals. Like so many other ghosts, he whispered constantly — not for Kathryn to join him, not to indulge her disillusionment, but so that, when she is close enough, dancing like this, he could thrust her back into the world again, force her to look at herself and to endure.

And so this Friday night seems somehow different. She has accepted that there is no one coming back for her. There is a quiet difference to her solitude now. She crumples the cardboard pizza boxes that the kids have left on the dining room table and carries them out to the garbage can. There is no resentment in her loneliness tonight, although she feels alone. Alone and strong. She drops the boxes on the porch. Leaning against the railing for support, she does a small pirouette and catches the railing again. Then she skips down the sidewalk, holding the cardboard boxes against her chest.

The Death of a Husband

LISTEN. I MIGHT AS WELL TELL YOU FROM THE START: I no longer believe in Romance. It's a plot designed to keep us chained to the same lifelong partners, to grease the wheels of capitalism, to keep us buying, buying, buying. And I know that you don't really buy any of those feeble plots that limp miserably across your television screen, the kind that send you dashing to the refrigerator during commercials in search of more genuine sustenance and comfort. Even there you are confronted by heart-shaped boxes of stale chocolate and overripe camembert that call for someone else's fingers and a bottle of heavy Bordeaux. I mean, really, life is nauseating enough without seeking out some ersatz hero who breathes heavily on the late night show and glares suggestively at his female sidekick.

Admit it: what really turns you on these late evenings is death. You've plotted your husband's at least a hundred times. Not the actual details. You're not into murder, of course, unless it's a good murder mystery, and then it always has to be someone else's. No, it's his absence that you find titillating, and the funeral itself. And all that money from the insurance company. I dare you to deny this: you even know exactly what you'll wear at his funeral. You've pictured yourself in black, looking forlorn but mysterious, sexy even, standing by the side of his grave, over and over. The setting is vaguely misty, just enough to give it that soft-blur focus. You will be the perfect spectacle of the bereaved, in your long flowing black cape and the stunning black fedora that covers just half of your face.

You picked out the underwear some time ago, your best black lace high-cut French panties, the ones he gave you for your birthday several years ago, the ones that wait at the back of your drawer between sachet bags of lavender. The kind that you perpetually hope will give you that seamless, sleek look: no hooks, no snags, no catches, nothing to interrupt the smooth gaze of the eye, as promised. Some haunting feeling prevents you from selecting them on a regular basis, as if you were saving them for a special occasion. Like the seduction scene you replay in your imagination every time you envision yourself wearing them. In this scene, you have on your best black stockings too, or maybe your white ones, the kind that are so sheer and so expensive that they would run all over the place the moment you put them on in real life.

This fantasy is a reversal of the night when you met him, the night when you lay in your tepid bathwater, debating whether or not you should even go to the party. How bloated you felt, how tired, too lazy even to shave your legs ("I'll be wearing trousers anyway," you thought). "I'll just stay for one glass of wine, then come right home and get a good night's sleep," you said, as you reached for your oversized white cotton briefs. You know the ones I mean: the underwear your mother ordered from the Eaton's catalogue for you when you were in grade ten, with the elastic all stretched out, but they never seem to wear out, and they're so damned comfortable that you cannot bring yourself to throw them out. On that night, despite your mortification, he never seemed to notice what you were wearing, but from that moment forward, you vowed to choose black over white, the future over the past, the unknown over the known.

You see what I mean. About the romance and consumerism crap. And this craze for striking parallels, as if our whole lives were bound up in finding perfect symmetry. Next you'll be wanting a happy ending to this story. Give me a break! Anyway, this is a story about death.

Back to the funeral: there you are, standing so wearily, holding back your tears, looking so lovely and vulnerable, while all your friends gather about you with an endless litany about love, death, life and other profundities.

The usual sort of banal soliloquies that people utter to satisfy themselves when they are hungry to speak. But there is one tall, rather attractive man in the crowd, a former cohort of your husband's, who approaches you and says absolutely nothing, merely clasps your hand tightly, looks you in the eye searchingly for what seems an eternity, and then ...

Honestly, you're so prurient and predictable, waiting there. Drooling for the details of someone else's sordid fantasy. You're either all a bunch of hopeless romantics (I noticed how your hearts were thumping away back there, as if mere words could restore the lustre to your pathetic love lives), or you're silly degenerates who have not yet caught on to the fact that romance and the author are dead, that in this age of Velcro, zippers no longer get inconveniently stuck, and closure has become a moot point.

The point here is that you do want him gone from your life, and dead seems the only way to do it. For the entire following day, you are lost in the details of your new life. You envision long, drawn-out afternoons over cups of aromatic, freshly roasted coffee, when your time is completely your own. No interruptions. True Independence. Glorious Self-Sufficiency. All that space to yourself, the luxury of solitude. You have long ago separated the possessions you value from his, determined what you could get for his Harley, sold off all his toys for imaginary sums, given away what you consider

his junk to the Salvation Army. The living room expands
in your head, the bedroom already seems tidier without
any of his clutter. You have remodelled the kitchen in a
new colour scheme, dispensed with those hideous shelves
he built for you "as a temporary measure only," indulged
yourself in multitudinous and varied extravagant sensa-
tions. You picture yourself taking strolls through your
favourite district, stopping at cafés whenever the whim
should sweep you away. No mandatory meals. No regular
sleep patterns. In fact, no clocks. And if you should choose,
the occasional lover between your sheets, who will always
leave early and never complicate your life with his insis-
tences, his demands to know how things between the
two of you will end up. For it is a fact that many in that
crowd will consider you a heroine, admire your stoic
patience. How beautifully you hold up under such duress!
What a tragedy! Such a young widow, with four children
to raise all on her own! ...

But wait a minute! Is that his car you hear coming up
the driveway? His key in the lock? In a panic, you scramble
aound the kitchen, adjust the silverware, place the wine
on the table, set the garnish delicately on the salad dish,
slip the plates into the oven to warm. Such reveries have
made you famished, inordinately greedy, anxious to please.
The candles are lit, and the flame mocks the surrounding
darkness. Like magic, his face appears before yours as
you encounter one another like intimate strangers, in
that warm, familiar way ...

Enough drivel. After all, we know how long your private dinner will last before the procession of kids comes barging in. We also know who it is who will be stuck in the kitchen, scraping that candlewax off the linen, washing those dishes, digesting that hoard of complaints about brown-bag equality ("Well, if he gets peanut butter cookies, how come I only get a banana? It's not fair"). And your beloved skillfully avoids confrontation through his long-standing technique of sprawling out on the chesterfield and turning up the volume on the hockey game, the organ chords chanting their tireless refrain beneath the commentator's agitated but controlled analysis. Even hours later, the kids all miraculously asleep, their whining rhythms curiously echoed in the jarring stillness, there is a longing that you cannot quite put your finger on. Even as you tug him toward you, ignoring his protests that the Leafs are actually ahead, that you may be witnessing history in the making, you recognize that something rare is transforming your spirit. A crisis of faith. And look at the bewilderment in his eyes when you lead him to the bedroom, where you have lit dozens of tiny candles in random patterns on the bureau, the night-stand, even the floor. Is it guilt that arouses your ardour now? You stroke that pale brow, that warm flesh, and chastise yourself inwardly for having imagined this body cold and six feet under. And who can blame you if you believe you hear the orisons of the cherubim and the seraphim when you cry out, Oh God?

Yes, something unearthly has possessed you. You cannot fall asleep after, in spite of the reassuring rhythm of his snoring. You pace back and forth in the kitchen, stare mournfully out the window at the waning moon. Then you retreat beneath the covers, where you find him once more and shape his astonished sleeping form to your pleasure. His breathing nearly regular until his lashes flutter and he stammers, "My God, you are going to kill me!" You are almost reduced to a fit of passionate weeping.

Finally, somewhere in the nascent hours of the morning, as the light outside begins to overtake the darkness at a compelling speed, your memory sifts mental photographs, takes stock of cherished experiences, replays in slow motion and then in inexplicably hastened flashes, those moments you have hoarded like shiny pennies. Slows to a halt at one. When was it? Fourteen years ago? Can't be. Yes. All of you were there: the picnic basket of sandwiches from the deli, the buttery cheese, the silky chartreuse grass, the smell of such indefinably sharp, pulsing colours, too strong to be real, almost hearing the sizzle of the sun on the back of your neck, how pungent and rusty the moist black earth smelled as you sat with him, leaning against a tree whose bark was born of a texture neither of you could accurately describe, though it teased the tips of your tongues. The photograph now fading to black and white, its stark colours absorbed into the salt-and-pepper of the TV screen's effervesence, as you slide heavily and pleasantly into that tingling state that precedes sleep.

Only the afterglow of the picture remains, as when you turn off the tube abruptly and a white ghost lunges off the screen at you, its distorted shape larger than life before it disappears entirely. Only the silhouette lingers behind the lids of your eyes, but you can distinguish quite clearly the outlines of two figures: you and your beloved, strolling hand in hand through that first day of spring, and onward into eternity.

After Hours, After Years

IT IS NOW MANY YEARS SINCE I HAVE SEEN HIM. Twenty, to be precise, for this summer marks the anniversary of our encounter in France. Only tonight when this Ontario summer humidity twists my unclothed flesh like an unwelcome blanket, when my tongue is thick and parched with memory, does his image return to haunt me. A trick of the moonlight spilling through the venetians and patterning the corridor, stark contrasts, ribbed shapes of blindness and light.

Not that I desire to be with him again, except in the abstract. Some kind of idealized lover who might inspire my daily life, or define by contrast the piquancy of the remembered past. Someone who might remind me that I am still one unto myself, unpossessed. No, I am happy, content, married to a man whose steady gaze keeps me peacefully anchored, whose rhythms blend harmoniously with mine.

And yet. His name slips out of me unbidden, murmured in half-sleep. Aziz. The syllables resonate with the nostalgia of a sensual summer, the soft hum of cicadas along the back streets of Nice, the city of escape. A Mediterranean summer, the Marché aux Fleurs overflowing with jonquils, violets and the ripe birds of paradise, obscene in their naked beauty. It is as if I am still lured by Aziz down unknown alleyways, clasping his warm hand. In the old city, he and I are enticed by the rich scents of onion pizzas sold by street vendors, amused by the multicoloured laundry flapping in the sea breeze. Wandering along the Promenade des Anglais in the late afternoon, we marvel at the living carpet of oil-slicked bodies, sun-worshippers who pass the day "on the rocks." (How little I knew then of politics, Aziz. To think that each of those flagstone steps along the promenade was constructed by exhausted French peasants, at the bidding of the rich English residents who were annoyed at the failure of their orange crops that season. Idle Victorian aristocrats, grown bitter without the luxury of citrus, determined to make everyone else equally acrimonious.) The four-mile-long boulevard is interrupted by islands of palms and carnations that obstruct our passage and bring us to breathtaking halts in speech. One day we visit the wealthy villa that we sight from the quay, now the Musée Masséna, where we laugh for an hour at the ridiculous representation of Napoleon as a Roman

Caesar. From here, the eastern part of the boulevard becomes the Quai des États-Unis, where the best restaurants jut out their culinary chins at us.

Tonight in Ontario, I can hear cicadas again, in the deep of summer. Tonight I am spiralled backward into our time together, the solemn wandering of backstreet *pensions* where matronly faces emerge from obscure windows and leer at the two of us, but deign to address only me: *"Mais lui, il n'est pas français."* The implication in those narrow-set eyes, nostrils flaring in condescension, that I am a whore of the lowest sort. Answered by angry sparks in the eyes of Aziz, his silence more ominous than any reproach, as yet one more door is closed to us. Even when we decide to gamble our precious funds and offer a tip, a bribe, the reply comes back the same: *"Pas de chambres. C'est la saison touristique."* And finally, we repose on a park bench, where rich women walk their manicured poodles, and it becomes clear that I shall have to rent a room on my own, sneak him in after dark. The thief of my dreams. Hours of waiting for him to appear, sadness and liquor on his breath, to finally wrap his warm skin around mine, to whisper between the sheets. Conspirators, giggling like children in the dark. Afterward, I creep down the hallway to the bathroom, a towel draped sarong-like around my hips, his shirt flung loosely over my goosefleshed arms, sleeves flapping like stunted wings. The warmth of my satisfied skin, the chill of the bare tiles. And the Mistral, far off in the night, the *sâcré vent* that the French love to blame for all their ills, howling beyond the massive slab stone walls that shield us by dark. Thinking, I am tasting the sands of Africa, as the grit scrapes my teeth in the morning.

At first they said it was because of his name. *Un étranger.* The wicked ironies of names: mine French, but Canadian, diluted over two centuries. I am from far away, alienated. He is Algerian, from a country worthy of French occupation but never French recognition. Three generations his family has laboured for them here in France, three generations of sweat, the same sweat I taste on his skin each night as the cobalt sky closes over the red and pink wounds of the sun. *Un étranger:* even to me, never having comprehended until too late the depth of his passion. Or maybe pride.

To each other we are strangers in the flesh only briefly. I begin my journey across the ocean toward his body in complete innocence. As a scholarship student in Toulon, I am fleeing the predictable grid of Canadian summer roads in favour of the paths I weave through the words of Rimbaud and Baudelaire. Aziz is a doctoral student in economics at the same university. Later, after we have touched one another finally, made indelible marks upon each other's skin, he discusses his theories and predictions with me as we lie on the beach, drinking a litre of dark Alsatian beer that has gone flat, and passing a cigarette back and forth between our fingers, then between our lips. He takes deeper drags from the cigarette than I do, so the cigarette is always overheated by the time he returns it to me. It is for pleasure that he studies, Aziz assures me (this is the summer we vow never to do anything but for the pleasure of it), since no one in France will ever hire, let alone take seriously, the predictions of an Arab economist. He turns away slowly as he says this, shielding his eyes that narrow into oblong slits at the periphery, to encompass the line where horizon and sea meet. The depth of his brown eyes straining to absorb all that blue.

But at the beginning of this particular summer, before the colour blue threatened to engulf us entirely, he works as a cashier in the cafeteria where I take my morning meal, and we make small talk as I pay for my croissant and *café au lait.* This is how we meet. Hushed exchanges over the aromatic steam of coffee and freshly baked breads. I must have made my decision then. Watching him eat his breakfast, slowly and meticulously, with long and elegant fingers, obviously enjoying his food. A man totally absorbed in the present. (When did I invent that rule for myself? The one that allows me to determine whether or not to make love with a man only after observing the way he eats. Men who consume in five minutes meals I have taken hours to prepare I dismiss easily. Men who wolf down and do not really taste their food, who are methodical or indiscriminate or indifferent in their appetites, will never be good lovers. The ones who are overindulgent will also think too much of their own pleasures in bed. But watch out for the ones who offer to share morsels from their plate with you, or who feed you with their fingers, whose lips smack in appreciation! My litmus test: bedroom manners follow table manners; it has not failed me yet.)

Besides his work in the cafeteria, Aziz has other work that allows him to cross my path and occupy my thoughts. Having associated Aziz with melting butter and warm kitchen smells, this startles me initially. I note that he also drives the bus that has been hired by my professor to escort our class to a small local museum. He is engaged for other menial tasks. Later he explains to me that he has been unable to find full-time work over the summer, and combines several part-time jobs in order to save for his studies in the autumn.

One day when I return from the beach where I have been suntanning and reading, Aziz is sitting languidly on the stoop outside the cafeteria following his afternoon shift. Words come easily to both of us at first, and then there is a long pause where we can only stare at one another awkwardly, then cast our eyes to the ground. Nervously, I excuse myself, saying I must shower off the salt from my skin and change for dinner. He says he is also heading for the showers, and sighs deeply. "Why don't we shower together?" I ask. (Where do these spontaneous outbursts originate?) He glances up from the steps quickly, as if to make sure I am not making fun of him. I am not sure myself if I'm joking or not, until I read his eyes. Then

suddenly we cannot leave there soon enough: Aziz toward
the workers' residence and I toward the women's. We have
agreed to meet in the shower in my complex. I cannot
remove my clothes quickly enough, fumbling with
buttons, shaking sand from my sandals and bathing suit.
When we clasp each other under the shower, it is as if we
have always known each other, as if soaping each other's
flesh were a cherished act of familiarity. His hands cup me
under the base of my spine as he swings me toward him
and presses me against the wall, and suddenly we are children discovering a new rhythm, riding a teeter-totter, his
strength lifting me high into the air with a breathtaking
suddenness before I am lowered back into clouds of steam.
By sheer dint of will, my thighs pushing down, I tip my
pelvis back and encounter his resistance with a thud that
sends me back up, the lovely sensation of being propelled
through air, suspended above the floor. When the ride is
over, the ground seems too close, too slippery, and there is
an explosion of stars below. Other flashes: white suds on
his brown skin. And after, in my room, his dark lashes
tinged with what look at first glance to be tears, but I
realize later are only water droplets. The laugh of his
strong white teeth emerging from his full lips. It is the
texture, the fullness of those lips, all that was never
uttered, that haunts me now. The heat of summer, slick
on our bellies. If cicadas could speak.

For weeks after this first encounter, I smuggle Aziz
into my room after hours and we lie together on my

cramped iron cot. My studies are deteriorating. In bed we read my books of poetry together, and my real French improves under his gentle instruction; he laughs at my mispronunciations of various slang words, and teaches me expressions that would make my professor blush. Afterward we sleep on my balcony, where it is slightly cooler, a sheet soaked in the water from my basin draped over our bodies, or lie there smoking cigarettes and drinking cheap red wine when the heat is too over-whelming. One night, as I lie wilted and drifting into sleep, he looks at me and says in rapid-fire French, "So, what is this for you? Am I some kind of trophy for you? Tell me, do Arabs fuck the same as Canadians?" I am stunned by his anger, summoned from my sleep by the sharpness of such unjust accusations. And while I am still trying to formulate the words to calm him, he pulls me on top of him, burying his rage inside me. Slowly this fades until we make love with an undefined sadness. After we cease tonguing one another to dispel the melan-choly, silence descends upon us, and by the morning all trace of his outburst has disappeared. Nothing is mentioned about it ever again, and after several days I pretend to have forgotten it happened at all.

What thrills me most about being with Aziz is his indefinable sense of mystery, and his devotion to discre-tion. He refuses to touch me in public, will not even hold my hand. In fact, he barely acknowledges any relation-ship to me. Arab custom, he explains. Only vulgar people

make crass displays in public. (Aziz, Aziz, why did you
have to defer to custom, you who pride yourself on being
a renegade? Why could you not have told me the real
motives, your fears, how you wanted to feign invisibility,
the way your body recoiled, immobile, under the scrutiny
of the French? The same amber-toned body I know as
warm and supple beneath the sheets.) I leave him my key
under the pillow in the mornings as I slip out for classes,
so that he can lock the door behind him. At the cafeteria
for lunch, as I push my tray toward his cash register, he
slides the key under my serviette so deftly that his
movement is imperceptible to anyone but me. Returning
my change, he presses the coins into my palm, and his
fingers brush mine momentarily; in spite of the electricity that this sends through our skin, he manages to
avoid eye contact. At first I feel hurt by what I perceive to
be his coldness, or change of heart. Later I learn to delight
in the contrast between his public nonchalance and his
private fervour.

The summer proceeds deliciously, and I yawn in my
classes from lack of sleep. I am blissfully unconscious of
the rest of the world. My thighs and my neck bear small
bruises, and my legs barely transport me from the classroom back to my evenings with him. After hours. The
only hours of the day that matter to me anymore.
Although I am afraid to admit it, I am falling in love.
When I reveal my feelings to Aziz, he confesses that he
feels the same. These declarations propel us onto a new

level of passion, more unbearable than the first, and I am weak in the knees as I float back to the classroom after two hours of sleep, my belly alive and humming with his song. It does not seem possible that such love can end.

Five months before my arrival in France, I had planned a trip to Italy with my girlfriend Suzanne, and tomorrow she will be here to collect me. I think I will not be able to endure this interruption, as much as I want to spend time with Suzanne. When she arrives, I meet her at a café opposite the train station, and over coffee tell her I have fallen in love. At first she is delighted, asks eagerly for details, but can barely mask her disgust when she sees a man with coffee skin saunter over to our table. Once she had told me that she saw nothing wrong with interracial relationships, but now her face, seeing my joyful acknowledgement of Aziz, tells a different story. She greets him in a restrained manner and the evening proceeds awkwardly. Finally the three of us decide that Aziz will take the train to Nice to meet us the following week, and all three of us will have two weeks together in Italy, if he leaves his job early. That is when my hopes flare. That is when the trouble begins.

I spend a strained week in Nice with Suzanne. She leaves on her own for Italy. I will not go there now.

Aziz arrives at the train station in Nice, stepping out into the humidity and looking almost like a bewildered boy until he sights my face in the crowd. The weather is muggy, unbearably warm. It feels as though it will begin to rain, but never does. A premonition of fear haunts me, but is dispelled as soon as I feel his cheek against mine. It is true that we spend many happy hours in the Chagall museum in the hills of Cimiez above the city. And that we are gifted with an incomparable view of the Bay of Angels from the exquisite little gardens in the Franciscan museum where we visit the grave of Matisse. We feel rich because entrance to museums in Nice is free and our pocketbooks are growing thin. But we remain trapped inside our tiny room until midmorning, the heat already soaring. By then we will be certain that the corridor will be clear of the proprietor, who might detect the presence of Aziz. As we linger late into the night in the darkness of cheap bars, thick with smoke or the fumes from the *marc* imbibed by old men, something steals in upon our joy. What seems at first to be a lighthearted affair becomes cumbersome with doubt and suspicion as the summer wears thinner on us.

One evening Aziz announces that we are going to visit some of his Arab friends on the outskirts of the city, insisting that he will go alone when I protest I am too tired after our day at the beach. I do not want to be apart from him, so reluctantly I agree to go. In a darkened bistro, I am introduced to several men, then ignored for the remainder of the evening, as the passionate cadence of Arab voices surrounds me. No one looks at me directly; I feel invisible. When Aziz finally indicates his readiness to depart, he flings his arms around me and pulls me toward the exit in what at first I believe is a sudden outburst of effusiveness. I am startled at this unusual display. After emotional farewells to all his *copains* (why then the customary refusal to be publicly demonstrative with me?), Aziz is sullen and uncommunicative. I feel as if I am being carted home, booty from a conquered town. Whereas, I realize with shame, I think of him as *my* prize, the exotic treasure I smuggle into my room by night. When I confront him with my anger at being treated like a toy, he flares, clenches his fists by his side and says nothing. But back in our bed, we are transported by the same waves repeating themselves, tides rolling across our flesh, ocean rhythms memorized by our senses from our daily pilgrimages to the sea. In spite of myself, I open to him like a sea lily, petal by petal. I marvel at the contrast between his dark limbs and my light skin as our bodies lie sleepily entwined.

In my dreams that night, I am falling, falling, yet I can neither reach the bottom nor swim up through endless layers of space to grasp the white net at the surface. When I break through the resisting net, I can still see nothing but darkness overhead. Struggling across vast distances, I cry out as I awaken, turn to Aziz for comfort. But his back is turned toward me, as sharply defined and unyielding in the moonlight as granite.

Tonight again the moonlight defines the granite lining the meandering creek that borders the property my husband and I have purchased. There are diamonds sparkling sinuously in the dark creek water that conjure up my memory of Aziz, of how many times we used to sit by the water's edge at night.

How we said goodbye no longer matters, for it was woven into our beginnings. I do remember how dignified he appeared as he turned to go, his strong face in profile, how he never hesitated nor looked back once, how swollen my flesh felt for weeks after we parted, how my thighs ached at the thought of him. It astounds me now that I have such clear memory pictures of that hazy summer, focused in spite of the obscuring heat, the cruelly brilliant glare of the sun. Neatly encased and labelled behind plastic in my photo album, the few actual photographs I have yield no mystery. The mental picture that I summon now, on this sultry summer evening, is unforgiving in its clarity and harshness: Aziz crouched over the glistening porcelain bidet, a parody of Rodin's *Thinker*, imitation bronze thighs and sinuous limbs, only the high, round moons of his buttocks caught white in the light spilling in from streetlamps. The degradation, the humiliation of that posture. He does not want to risk using the shared toilet in the hotel corridor, lest he be discovered. Aziz does not know that I am awake, nor that I observe him, and I take care that my body betrays no movement. I know that his feigned contemplation, his cautious silence, designed not to wake me, arises from his pride and another kind of beauty, one seldom praised in classical sculpture.

Now I can no longer look at Rodin without feeling my heart contract, without trembling with rage and love and a sadness so intense that it escapes articulation, gathering mutely at the back of my throat. Twenty years. Two full decades to reach this clarity. (My ignorance, my love.)

The air shimmers. It is scorchingly hot again tonight. Sleep is but one of the many unkept promises I made to myself. I wander to the edge of our property, which slopes down toward a creek bed and opens further out onto a pond. My feet make slurping noises as I glide across the grass; a low mist shrouds the pond like cotton wool. The water is prolific with insects that leap across its surface, leaving weblike patterns too dizzying to trace. My eyes close heavily, and I force them open. In the distance, cicadas sing a pulsating song so forlorn that I shiver and have to close my eyes again.

Open Skies

Vertical is pain.
Vertical is love.
But horizontal
to keep clean.
Horizontal
to lullaby.
From side to side to still the cry
To ease the ache to dull the pain
From side to side from side to side
Rocking and rubbing the women ride.
— Elizabeth Smart, "There Are
Two Movements in a Woman's Life"

I USED TO LIVE ON THE PRAIRIES, CLOSE TO THE foothills north of Calgary, in a teepee that I built myself.

I lived in that teepee for a year. Eventually I was able to withstand very cold temperatures, even the minus-forty Alberta winter, which was dry and cold, not burdened with dampness. I gave up using an alarm clock. Every morning at four minutes to six, a snowy white owl would flap its wings against the canvas at the apex of my teepee, perching itself on the narrowest pole where the lodgepole pines met and crossed. When you consider that snowy white owls have a wingspan of over four feet, you can imagine the sound of my morning wakeup call, feathers and quills against canvas. Yet I would stir slowly, reluctant to leave the warmth of my sleeping bag, and throw some kindling into the Quebec wood heater before bolting outside to fetch wood from the woodpile. Then I would jump back into my sleeping bag until the warm air inside the teepee roused my blood before I crawled out to put on my secretary clothes. Outside in the morning air, the owl would stare at me, as well it might: I looked out of place in my city clothes and would gladly have worn feathers instead. Snowy owls are endangered in Alberta, but I discovered a whole nest of them in the small forest nearby. That was a year of many such blessings.

In exchange for living on a rancher's land for free, I came home from work every day and moved his steers from one field to the adjoining one. I would keep an eye on them. I had read many stories in the papers about ranchers losing their cattle and understood why my surveillance was necessary. This was during the late seventies, when cattle rustling frightened many ranchers. But it did not frighten them nearly as much as the bizarre and inexplicable deaths of cows that were found dead in the field with no external markings on their flesh, their viscera and brains completely disintegrated. Scientists from Agriculture Canada came and went in their four-by-fours. Stories circulated of satanic cult worshippers, alien invaders and biological warfare, but no one ever solved the mystery of why so many cows should die in such a slow, cruel fashion. Nor could anyone understand how the hoofprints of the cattle seemed to be going toward the meadow and not out of it. It almost seemed that someone or something had forced them to march backward.

In spring and summer, I also ploughed between the fir trees that were planted in rows on the adjoining section of land, getting them ready for the next Christmas season. The rancher, who was really a gentleman rancher and hired all his farm help, gave me investment tips. He was a stockbroker in downtown Calgary and only appeared on the occasional weekend, strutting across the fields in his cowboy boots and ten-gallon hat, or riding a chestnut gelding. With no rent and little overhead, I invested nearly all of my pay until I'd stashed away enough to travel around the world, which is precisely what I did after I took my teepee down. I always believed that I could return to those days of wide blue cloudscape, open skies.

Because what I loved most about the long days I spent in the summer there, after I'd quit my city job and was forming my travel plans, was that sky, the endless sky, the sky that seems to alter with each mood shift. The clouds that rolled by, the sunrises that lit the distant mountain peaks a warm coral, or the sun slipping below the horizon and leaving the air suddenly cool and fragrant, leaving muted pastels stretched across the wide, wide canvas of the prairie. I have never found skies like that, anywhere. On full-moon nights, my friends would come over for a party and we would play glow-in-the-dark Frisbee, drink too much and trip in gopher holes as we ran and ran across the land, through those long summer nights wide with light. And some late afternoons were glorious: the newly mown grain swirled into stooks as wide as a big man's embrace, glowing in that peculiar olive and honey light that fills the air in the brief hour before dusk. At around the same time of day, I could sit on the edge of the coulee and watch the wind-rippled wheat announce a thundercloud come rolling in. From miles and miles away I would sight the foreboding cumulus as it strolled across an otherwise azure sky. I charted the progress of the cloud with forbearance, stoically certain that I could live with the elements. Usually the dark dome would arrive directly overhead, contract and release its rage, dumping rain all over me for five or six minutes until my clothes and sandals were drenched, and then pass on. I would follow it with my eyes, awed at its

power to alter the landscape so briefly and yet so dramatically, leaving in its wake only raindrops glistening weakly
in a pale light. The grateful earth absorbed the water
quickly, the dust settled momentarily and the smell was
iron-rich, startlingly sweet. I was impressed, awestruck,
beholden.

One day I peeled off all my clothes, let the rain wash
over me, feeling the brief cold shock as my nipples stood
on end and the hairs on my arms were raised. I wondered
if this was the craziest or the most inspired thing I had
ever done; either I would get pneumonia and die, or I
would feel renewed in the faith of my own recklessness.
Quite suddenly I felt overwhelmed by the sharpness of
everything, by the joy of being completely alone, and
I began sobbing. As I stood with my head tilted toward
the sky, water rolled off my forehead and into my ears;
I wasn't sure if it was rain or tears, and I didn't care.
Every pore of my being was open to that moment, and
nothing else mattered.

Now, many years later, I live on a foggy island. I wake
up to my alarm clock every morning, and I work at a
regular job, trying to make mortgage and car payments.
The rainforest grows darkly all around me. I breathe in
salt when I walk along the waterfront. Salt has its own
integrity, but it is not the same as prairie air on a late
summer's day. Recently I came to know that I would
have to leave my marriage of a dozen years, and the real-
ization arrived with the same eerie clarity as I had felt

watching that cumulus cloud creep across the sky. One night I stood in the emergency ward with my infant son in my arms, and thought he was dying. He had stopped breathing, gone limp, and his skin was burning against mine. Later I stood still as I watched him breathing inside the oxygen tent and for a moment its shape reminded me of my teepee, except that it was transparent and artificial. I knew in that moment I would die for that small boy, that I had already died a slow, cruel death. I knew that I had no one to share this with, that I was in the loneliest marriage in the world, that I had borne my children alone, and would raise them alone. These thoughts were as lucid to me as the bluest Alberta sky. The tempest rolling toward me had been within my sight for years, rumbling at a distance. For some time I had thought I might avert the storm or avoid it entirely if I merely changed my perspective. Now I saw that I would need to stand directly in its path and let it pass through me and then watch it move slowly past me.

Tonight I will tuck my children safely into their beds, and wave softly to the babysitter, curled up on the couch. I will go down to the Nanaimo River to visit my lover, following a highway that is alive, headlights pulsing in the darkness, foghorn accompanying me around the harbour. He lives in an old miner's cabin and the roof is covered with moss. I will be able to see the smoke from his woodstove as I turn off the highway. I will take heart from this. I will feel my wings expand

and my quilled feathers fill with air. We will sip whisky
from chipped porcelain cups that are marked "Esso Full
Service" in red and blue. His dog, the oldest and ugliest
dog I have ever seen, will start howling as soon as I come.
She will howl when he hits the wrong note on his
trumpet, and whimper as he puts the instrument back
in its case. He will tell me the story again of how he
found her as a puppy, how he carried her home inside his
jacket on his motorcycle, how he felt her friskiness
against his chest until the hum of the engine put her to
sleep. He will slowdance me around the room until I
have stopped crying. Later he will tell me that summer
is just around the corner, that he could feel it all day in
the air. That he can't wait to take me down to the pools
where he fishes and swims. That he will catch crayfish
and cook them for me in garlic and butter. And I will
believe him, because the fire will be nearly out and the
rain will have started coming down.

Riding to Tibet

The birds of flight return, crucified shapes
old deaths restoring vigour through the sky
mergent with earth, no more horizons now
no more unvisioned capes, no death; we fly.
            — *Muriel Rukeyser, "Theory of Flight"*

JOAN WRAPS ONE ANKLE AROUND HER LEG, AND
John is reminded of morning glory twisting itself around
the stalks of plants: resolute, intrepid, inescapable. She is
limber, tall and lithe, and unable to sit still. Like a blue
heron staring ahead perpetually, wings' breath rippling
the water, oblivious to life below. She swivels her neck
toward him, but does not look at him. He remembers
how beautiful she was the day they met: her long, sleek

body oiled and dazzling by the side of the pool. She has grown even more elongated over the years.

The night has been blustery and chilly, rain whipping against the frame of the bathroom window and making it rattle. All three children are finally sleeping. Joan has made their school lunches, signed their permission forms, and now she breathes slowly and slumps her back against the bathroom wall.

John is soaking in the bathtub, making plans for the future, while Joan sits on the toilet seat, the "throne." They are drinking a Chilean Cabernet Sauvignon. Not a great year, but it warms them. Joan leans across the sink, and, slightly hunched over, reaches outside the windowsill to flick the ashes from her cigarette, a casual gesture that irritates her husband. She knows he dislikes it, so she makes an effort, however futile, to keep the smoke from reaching him. She places one sandalled foot on the toilet seat and leans her chin on her knee.

John is thinking about Tibet again. And about a poem he vaguely recalls in which a man rides the rails across the country, looking for work during the Depression. And about India, where there are still steam engines from the days of the Raj, perfect trains on perfect rails following an imperfect time schedule.

"It was just a matter of seconds," she says. "I wouldn't have had the same return if I'd waited any longer. It blows me away how important the timing is in this business. Everything in life is about timing, actually, isn't it?"

He doesn't answer. Her nervousness animates her entire body, comes from the ground below her, from the smooth bathroom tiling squares that he has painstakingly grouted. The energy rises up through her body, and her arm slices the air to emphasize what she is saying. John used to find this endearing, but now it seems to annoy him. He thinks about how he would describe himself in a cyber ad, just in case there was anyone out there in cyberspace who could read him; he could say he had a placid nature. "Lazy" is what Joan calls him. By her standards, anyone who doesn't get out of bed at four-thirty as she does is slothful.

A DAY TRADER ON THE STOCK MARKET, JOAN RISES early every morning to check the market activity on the Internet. On the West Coast, this means 4:30 a.m. It is her favourite time of day: dark, quiet, a pot of coffee beside her computer, and her body slowly waking up as she skims the latest reports. She uses the information from yesterday's newspapers, follows her hunches, tries to guess the economic trends of the day. She imagines herself to be a regular Nancy Drew. Minutes after she has finished entering her trade, Joan mutters to her imaginary colleagues, those other traders whose bids make the stock values rise and fall like waves. She gloats when she beats other investors to the punch, and curses when she misses an opportunity. Her blood is warmed by the excitement. By seven, when she pours the final sip of coffee into her cup and heads outside to observe the sun rising over the garden hedge, she feels fully alive, one ear cocked to hear the children heading for the bathroom. The rest of the day tries her patience; she is not the best stay-at-home mom, though she admires those friends of hers who seem to love the job. She listens to the birds chirping, turns her mind to the more practical aspects of the day. What to take out of the freezer to thaw for dinner, how many minutes she has before she has to prepare breakfast for the troops. She has accomplished something. A feeling of peace descends over her that is in marked contrast to the bursts of adrenalin she experiences when hunched over her computer, the panic when she isn't certain she can sell or buy before the whole picture changes irrevocably.

Maybe the most pleasure she gets from her work is from the flip side of the panic. And never having to battle traffic or leave the sanctuary of domestic bliss that is her home, the home she has created and in which she can move around whenever she needs a break. She likes the sense of time stretching out infinitely ahead of her as she surveys the greenness of her garden, the clouds heralding the day's weather.

Joan has tried to explain this to John, but he doesn't get it. He mocks her for being a "capitalist exploiter." Not that he objects when she wins big. He is certainly not unwilling to share in the spoils. Recently she cleared over thirty-four hundred dollars on pork bellies in one day and they decided to use the money to pay off their Visa card. Pork bellies — what a cliché! But she had been right: consumers were afraid of mad cow disease. Afraid of hormones in their poultry. So all that was left for carnivores was the other kind of white meat. She laughs out loud again, wondering what pigs would make of this, whether they felt it in their guts, as she did. What a bizarre world we live in, she thinks, not for the first time.

TODAY SHE DID WELL ON THE MARKET — NO, more than well, she was fantastic. Tonight she is exhilarated, especially after losing money and enduring John's teasing when she said last week that she felt lucky making the move into the commodities market. It reminds her of diving when she was younger. Of standing on the high board, uncertain whether she would slip perfectly into the water or do a belly flop. What she really remembers is the rush up her spine, the tingling in her legs, the thrill of anticipation. The dive itself was secondary. Last week John had rubbed it in. Told her, over and over, that she had belly-flopped again, that she was bound to get depressed being engaged in such risky work. Ever since their youngest son Ryan's birth, John encouraged her to find more steady work, has suggested the CGA exam. But the thought of becoming an accountant makes her nauseated.

How can he lecture her about ideal jobs, never having had one himself? He's never had an income. John has been working on his doctorate in microbiology for eleven years, since before the children were born. Joan thinks it unlikely that he'll ever finish now. He says there is no point, since he isn't going to do industry-based research. He talks about the importance of "pure" research, of doing "real" science. As if it were a border he were protecting from invasion. How he expects to do anything at all is a moot point until he has finished his degree, but this does not stop him from sanctimoniously berating his colleagues, whom he says have already "sold out." He does this regularly, but over after-dinner drinks when they have friends over, his tone is more moderate. He takes Luke to task for this.

"How is life in the corporate world, Luke? I wish I had a regular paycheque right now." After their guests have left and they are gathering up the empty bottles from the table, John will ridicule Luke behind his back. Likely he will remind Joan that Luke had been "pussy-whipped" by his wife Terri into accepting a job at a petrochemical firm instead of finishing his doctorate.

"Actually, it's not so bad," concedes Luke, taking a long draw on his beer bottle. "The politics can be pretty thick, but so far I've managed to stay clear. You know, the regular nine-to-five routine has its advantages. I was never able to get away from thinking I should be reading or writing the damn thesis, twenty-four hours a day, but now, when I come home for supper, I can just tune out the work and relax. Quit thinking about it. No more guilt, you know what I mean? I guess I would have finished the dissertation eventually, but my heart wasn't in it."

"What about the guilt of what they're going to do with your research? Do you have any control over that?" asks John.

"I try not to spend too much time thinking about that." Luke steals a look at Terri out of the corner of his eye. "You know, we all have to give up some control somewhere, sell out on some level. Even grad school was like that, sucking up to the right profs, changing my stats to apply for whatever grant I needed, that kind of shit."

"Yeah, but it's different if where that material goes is still within your power," John retaliates. "I mean, nobody does much about it until you publish it, and then most of the time it's for academic discussion. You don't have to prostitute yourself in the same way as you do when some corporation owns you."

Joan suspects she is among those whom John would claim prostitute themselves for money. But he was connected to her and to their children by accepting that money, she thought, a thread he grasped at often enough when he needed it. More like an apron string than a thread, she thought unkindly. Not that she would dare point that out to him, especially when he was drinking.

THE MEMORIES OF THESE DINNER PARTIES NOW flash through her mind uncomfortably as she watches him lather his chest in the bathtub. John sips his wine and inhales the sandalwood scent from the soap bar propped on his belly; he examines the glistening swirl of hair and bubbles pooled in his navel. "I wonder if I'll ever get to travel again," he muses out loud. "I still remember how much more spontaneous my life was before the kids were born. I actually used to imagine that Tibet was within reach, that I would be going there next year or something." But how can he have a serious conversation about Tibet with his wife, a woman whose agitation prevents her from enjoying a long, meditative soak, whose nervous energy exhausts him even at this moment? Joan says nothing. She lights another cigarette.

"You don't see what I mean, do you? I guess asking you to take the long view isn't really fair. Especially from a nearsighted woman!" he laughs. If they were really in tune spiritually, she would be able to read his thoughts right now. There would be no need for speech. "Maybe some day we won't even have to talk. We'll have grown so used to each other that speech will be unnecessary."

"John, what a horrid thought!"

"I think it's wonderful, actually."

Joan turns her thoughts to more mundane matters. "Ryan's wetting his bed again," she says. "I can't believe it, I thought we were through with all that. He's been toilet-trained for months now, but he's too lazy to get out of bed in the morning to go to the toilet. And when he does make it to the bathroom, he misses the toilet every time." Joan rubs her eyes in fatigue. She can feel her energy fading suddenly, realizes it is but a few brief hours until she has to get up.

She would understand nothing about my yearning to take yak butter tea with peasants, thinks John, nor how much I want to make a pilgrimage up the slopes of Lhasa. In his mind, he can see the crust of snow along mountain peaks that appear calm in the morning light. He dreams of a final stage in the journey, unimpeded by the chatter of human voices. He would like to describe to her what a long, slow ride it will be up the trails to the temple, what they will have to endure in order to arrive at their destination: the thinning of the air, the bitter cold, the gruelling hike across rocky terrain. He has studied all the photographs of Lhasa, and is entranced by the strange landscape, the striated clouds above vertically thrusting rocks, as if all of nature were pointing to the sky, topped by shrines, the dome-shaped chorten with their spiralling roofs.

But she would not understand. Nor would she encourage him if he were to tell her that he longs to paint the canyons approaching what he has imagined as the gates to heaven.

In his next life, he will be a painter, he thinks. Not a scientist. John has dreamed of going to Tibet since his first year at university, when he met a Buddhist in his chemistry class. Within a few weeks, they'd become good friends, both young men engaging in heated philosophical debates over Vietnamese soup every Friday night at a small cheap restaurant.

"One day we'll go to Tibet," he says. From her startled look in response, he realizes he has not been listening to her describe her frustrations with Ryan. Her stories seem the same every night.

Reminded by his mention of Tibet, Joan obviously wants to tell her story about meeting the Dalai Lama in McLeod Ganj all over again. As if he could not predict every turn of phrase in the well-worn, well-rehearsed story she drags out every time someone admires that goddamn rug in their bedroom. She's lost in her own little world, describing her trip to India of years ago, just before she'd met John. She knows he's heard all this before.

"Do you remember I told you about meeting the Dalai Lama? It was the leader's birthday and he blessed the carpet I was having made, even though it was only half done. I can still remember its warp threads trailing onto the dusty road where some of the women had dragged it for the procession."

It gives Joan immense pleasure to contemplate the carpet, which now lies in the bedroom. She has done her yoga exercises on it every morning for fifteen years, her fingers tracing the intricate mandalas that swirl in delicate patterns across the dark blue border.

"Do you remember, John, how it arrived at our apartment with a hundred and four stamps on it, no customs stickers, no duties paid, no post office notice to come and pick it up?" Numerous packages she'd sent home from India had either not arrived, or had been torn open and their valuable contents removed. She had nearly given up hope of seeing the carpet again, assuming it to be lost in the post. Joan always associates the carpet with the Dalai Lama, because she had shaken his hand, part of the birthday procession of well-wishers. Only a week before he had arrived there for the birthday celebrations, she had commissioned the carpet that she had asked him to bless. She recalls him laughing that it was only half woven. His laughter was childlike and infectious, rising from his belly.

"He seemed to look right through me. I couldn't take my eyes off him. And then he laughed again at the carpet. It was all rolled up, with its wool threads sticking out. He asked me what I would use it for." She puts her wineglass on the sink countertop and sits back down on the toilet. She would like to light another cigarette, glances at the package of Number 7s on the back of the toilet, and wills herself not to. Joan remembers thinking she wanted the carpet to make love on. Before she met John.

Her mind drifts back to the day when she went to visit the carpet makers in Dharamsala. What a special day!

She had climbed the forested hill, following the path that was dotted with piles of stones and prayer flags. Through the trees below, she could see the monks, young boys in ochre robes, playing tag as their laughter carried up the hillside. Eventually she came to a weather-beaten wooden building in a clearing near the top of the hill. There were loud thumping noises and laughter emerging from the open windows, but she could not locate the carpet factory. She peered anxiously through the entrance door and saw the looms, the source of the clacking noises. What had she been expecting, an industrial site?

Before she could recover from her surprise, a woman with a wrinkled face and a grin full of bad teeth came toward the door, chattering in Tibetan, and pulled her inside. Joan looked around for someone younger, in the hope that her English would be understood. There were children who were making carpets alongside the women. They all stopped work to make her tea and stroke her hair. None of them objected to her interrupting their work, nor did they make her feel that they were in a hurry to return to their looms. The women gave her their babies to hold. Sun filled the room, illuminating the dust. Shrill singing continued loudly in the pauses between conversation; no one seemed to mind the language barrier. Joan watched the ancient looms resting in sunlight, noting that there were no windows, just openings in walls. Again raucous laughter filled the air as a toddler peed on his mother's skirt. She ran out the door with him still spraying in an arc, holding him at arm's length, as if it were a game and he were winning.

None of the babies wore diapers. She had not burdened John with this final detail when she once described the memorable day to him; he washed his hands nearly as often as Howard Hughes, she thought, and would be horrified to hear about the poor sanitary habits of the people in the village. It would change his elevated opinion of Tibetans — an opinion she had given him to believe was the right one, had supported and romanticized each time they discussed the possibility of going to Tibet someday. Who knows what John really thought?

Joan thinks of the harried mothers she encounters in the aisles of the drugstore, buying packages of disposable diapers that cost more than most of the mothers look like they can afford. She rarely sees the look of contentment that she observed on the faces of the Tibetan women as they worked at their looms, nor does she hear people singing as they work in the relaxed manner she had seen that day.

"You know, I think those carpet makers have the best jobs in the world. I've never seen people seem so satisfied with what they were doing, so happy. Nobody was in a hurry to do anything."

John is twirling the soapy hairs on his belly. He's heard this comment before, wonders why she keeps repeating it. She loves these generalizations. Maybe her work is finally getting to her. He thinks of the lists she

makes in her day planner, rigidly organizing each hour of
every day. She has to learn to let it flow, he thinks to
himself. Or get into raising the kids with a little more
enthusiasm. He cannot tell her that he thinks going to
Tibet will save him somehow, that the cold air will clear
something out of his mind that has been clouding his
thoughts for years, wipe out a childhood that made him
believe in fear. She would mock him for idealizing something about which he had no understanding. Tell him,
as she had once, that he had no right to romanticize the
conquest of an untouched country, imagining that his
troubles would "melt like lemon drops" once he set foot
on the snows of the Himalayas. Yet, naïve though it
sounds, he still believes this to be true. Out loud he says,
in what he hopes is a cheerful, distracted voice, "Sounds
like you should move to Dharamsala and make carpets."

Joan splashes him with water, partly because she's
annoyed that he's not been listening. But she's also tired.
She glimpses her imagined Tibet, but only in short bursts,
like the small energy bursts that impel her through her
days. Right now it seems as elusive to her as the big break
on the gold market that every investor dreams of making
just before retiring. If gold drops by ten cents tomorrow,
she should make a buy.

Joan is not planning a journey to Tibet. She and John
read numerous books about Tibet together, lying in bed
side by side on winter afternoons, before the children
were born, when they believed themselves in love, when

they called themselves soul twins, marvelling at the
coincidence that their names were identical but for one
letter. She thought of him then as her double, imagined
an invisible strand attaching them together so that they
were always connected, even when he was away. All the
moments they spent together dreaming about Tibet,
about a future that stretched beyond their present lives,
have become woven together in her mind, so that she
can barely remember their sequence in real time. She
imagines going to Tibet someday, but only a fool would
believe that salvation rests upon completing the actual
journey. It doesn't matter to her whether she actually
goes or not. Joan believes that her own journey will take
her to the same place in the end. She says this to John,
who laughs. She tells him about other things she
believes in. She believes in the continuity of love. As she
believes that fidelity has nothing to do with the genitals,
but with the more dangerous organ of the heart.

FIVE YEARS LATER, JOAN WILL THINK ABOUT THIS
again when John announces to her that he has met a
woman who will allow him to "follow his spiritual
path" and not hold him back as Joan has done, and she
will feel her heart constrict. Perhaps she should have
been planning a journey after all, she thinks now. Perhaps
she should have listened more seriously to his dreams
about going to Tibet. Perhaps focusing on the business of

making a living was useless in the end. Where had it gotten them? There are some cruelties that have no name, she will think. For the last few years, Joan has had no touch from John, other than the lash of his criticism, which has become more pronounced. She has made light of it, joked about it, but mostly prefers not to think about it anymore. She has combed through all the photographs, and found none of the two of them standing together or touching; John was always out of the picture.

When John leaves her, five years later, he will say it is because she's too jittery, and because he cannot envision going to Tibet with her. She will remember that evening of long ago, watching him lying in the bath, the smells of sandalwood and wine filling the small bathroom. He has begun to consider the journey more seriously, he will say. She will watch in stupefaction as John takes almost all of the furniture — even the new freezer, which she has filled with painstakingly labelled and dated plastic freezer bags of produce from their garden. Ryan will stare at his father and cry because his Popsicle supply is being carted off. She will imagine John taking out a package that says "Strawberries, June 1996" in her handwriting to defrost it for his lover's breakfast. When he packs his clothes and personal belongings, he will take all the books she has given him about Tibet, and several that he gave to her. She will watch him load them in his meticulous fashion, spine down, in the cardboard boxes he has brought home from the liquor store, and suddenly the full symbolic impact of what he is packing up will move her to tears of rage.

"You can't take all those," she will stammer, her words choking in her throat. She sees the Tibetan carpet rolled up beside one of the cardboard boxes, and tears spill down her cheeks.

"Oh, so now you're going to start taking back presents. Pretty childish, Joan." Refusing to look at her, John will continue pulling books off the shelf in their bedroom, including those by Alexandra David-Néel, a woman whom they both agreed was a fraud and an egotist, but who nonetheless was responsible for bringing the teachings of Tibetan Buddhism to the West. "A necessary conduit" was how John had once described her.

Joan will pick that book up out of the pile, open the pages at random, and read: "Mind and senses develop their sensibility in this contemplative life made up of continual observations and reflections. Does one become a visionary, or, rather, is it not that one has been blind until then?" She will note again, this time with a disdainful irony, the dedication on the frontispiece: "To my true love: Make the journey with me. Forever yours, John." And still on the shelf is the work of Heinrich Harrer, the German explorer of Tibet who would have his own ego crushed in the process of discovering Buddhist philosophy. Most treasured of the books she owned was *The Way of the White Clouds*, by Lama Govinda, which they had spent many hours reading to each other. John's back will be turned to her as he leans over the box arranging the books, and she will quickly thrust the tattered Govinda book under the pillow, her heart beating in rage. The rolled carpet she thrusts under the bed. He will leave her with the old bed, to be haunted by all its memories. Typical.

"The truth is, you never gave me any presents anyway. Fuck you, John. Take the books." He will not reply, but will intently fold the flaps at the top of the cardboard box.

Later that night, hot tears streaking her face, her limbs heavy and her heart sad, scarcely breathing, Joan will leaf through the book and fall asleep still wrapped in an old blue wool sweater. Just before sleep finally overtakes her, however, she will feel a tug above her navel and a weight being removed from her body. She will remember the book and realize that it has slipped off her chest and onto the floor, onto the rolled Tibetan carpet that protrudes from under the bed.

When Joan remembers him years later, it will be the memory of the day they drank wine in the bathroom, watching him rise dripping from the bath and leaning toward the towel rack, amphibious, seeking dry land. From her perch on the toilet seat she had rubbed him dry, along his back first; then she turned him around and dried the insides of his thighs where the hair ran in wet rivulets. She held his buttocks, parted them like wet melon halves under her palms. She put her finger in a corner of the towel and dried his scrotum, each hair springing back to life and turning a lighter colour when not matted with water. Where the foreskin would not pull back at her urging, Joan guided it free with her tongue. At the tip of his penis, John was weeping. And so she had cradled him like this between her lips, led him to their bed in the next room, taken him on that long slow ride across the ocean of their mattress, until he had said he felt reborn, as if he had been returned to himself after a long forgetting. On their bed, they had wanted to peel back each other's skin, rub each other raw, before they had both slipped back into the soothing safety of the bath water. And then once more they were moving forward together, in perfect time, the waves swishing rhythmically against the sides of the tub. They had laughed as they had mopped up the floor together afterward.

YEARS LATER, ON THE LONG TRAIN RIDE FROM Delhi, John will recall how it is her absence he once hungered for, the way he could imagine the emptiness of the house filling up with a fragrance that was at first strange and then familiar. He could lie on the bed, unstrap his watch, stare at the water marks on the ceiling, imagine her moving, and feel a weakness he did not like to admit. Now that they have parted, now that each of them has betrayed the flesh and blood of their old dreams, it is her presence he craves. He will remind himself that he has always liked being alone, and now as his new lover has decided that she could not accompany him to India, he has achieved the total quiet he missed when living with Joan and the kids. He will be on the train from Delhi, the seat beside him empty but for his paperback, splayed open at the spine. If she were here, John thinks, Joan would make him use a bookmark and not ruin yet another copy of *The Way of the White Clouds*. He will feel mildly irritated by the sweat rolling between his shoulder blades as he hangs his hat by a loose thread from its inside band on the clotheshook fastened to the train compartment wall. He will remember the smell of sandalwood soap when he comes across it again in India. He will remember bad Chilean wine. His eyes will hurt him suddenly. Blinded by the white midday light, shrinking from it, he will move to pull down the blind over the window. And then he will feel nothing at all. It will be disorienting at first, not being able to carry on the life to which he has been accustomed in his former dwelling-place. He will feel weightless. Beneath his body, the wheels will hum rhythmically across their tracks, vibrating like bedsprings.

Infant Colic: What It Is and What You Can Do About It

MOM HAS IT IN HER HEAD THAT WE NEED TO GO again this year. Even though my baby brother was just born two months ago and hasn't stopped crying since. Next time, she should try to get a baby that doesn't spit up either. Since those jerks in government have cut her daycare subsidy, she has to stay home now. Can't afford to work, she says. But she wants to have a little family holiday too, she told me. She says she's never missed the Folk Festival, so why should she this year? We're taking the ferry from the Island now. It's just pulling away when Tony finally falls asleep in his Snugli on my mom's chest, so she has her feet propped up on the seat across from the one she's sitting in, even though she always tells me never to do that myself. But she's nearly asleep, so I won't say anything to her right now. She must be really tired. Tony screams every day from afternoon until midnight. Oh my God! He has colic. I usually have to put myself to bed because she says she's knackered and I know she means it because she has tears rolling down her cheeks. "Sorry, honey," she always says.

Yesterday Mom was looking at me again with that "I-can't-believe-how-you're-not-my-little-girl-anymore" look out the corner of her eye, while she sat at the kitchen table, rubbing the side of the telephone and cradling the receiver between her neck and her shoulder. I hate it when she talks about me to her friends.

"She thinks I'm some kind of flake because I care about culture and travel and would really like to move all of us into something more community-oriented," Mom was saying on the phone to her best friend Suzie. I wasn't supposed to be listening, but I could hear from the kitchen, where I was washing the dishes. She's like, "The girl also thinks I'm her personal chauffeur and a Walking Wallet. Or some kind of Human Sponge." She had henna in her hair again and it was oozing out of the plastic bag she had clipped with a clothespin around her head; it was green all down the back of her neck. I hoped her old boyfriend would show up at the door again and surprise her like he did that one time. Or that the phone receiver slipped along her neck in the green ooze.

Mom insists that I travel with her to the Folk Festival in Vancouver every year. Even though I'm nearly thirteen and should be able to stay home by myself if I want.

Lauren and I got the babysitting course certificate last month, so I'm old enough to be by myself. We both took the classes together after school. I was good at burping babies; they even brought in a real one for us to practise on. Oh my God! You should've seen it. It was hilarious. I should be able to get lots of work, now that all the daycare centres are closing because they can't afford to run them anymore. So I figure I can get a bunch of kids to pick up from the elementary schools every afternoon after I finish my classes, and I should be able to make big bucks next fall.

Plenty of people are always giving my mom this advice on how to get rid of Tony's colic. They go, like, "Don't eat garlic, quit eating eggs, give up milk, it's spices in your diet, give him peppermint oil and burp him more." Our next-door neighbour said it must be because Mom really wanted a girl and doesn't really like Tony. It doesn't seem like such a big deal to me. I mean, it's not like he's like one of those starving kids with ribs showing like you see on TV ads. I bring him a hot-water bottle for his tummy at night, but it doesn't always calm him down. We've tried wrapping him up like a burrito in a flannel blanket too.

Ever since her boyfriend went back up to Alaska to work on the pipeline, Mom's been crying a lot, especially after Tony came. She thinks I don't understand how she got pregnant by mistake, even though she talks so loud on the phone with Suzie all the time. She goes, like,

"Dave can't make it home in time for the baby to be born. They're going into full production right then, so he'll be getting time and a half." I guess that has something to do with more money. Sometimes adults confuse me. Not only didn't I understand what she was talking about, but I didn't get why she was talking as if she was glad for him being away when she looked so sad. Sometimes I hear her on the phone with Suzie, who did the prenatal classes with her, and she goes, like, "lanugo" and "impetigo," so that I don't know what she's saying. But I did learn that Tony has a hole in his head called a "fontanelle" where he has this yellow flaky scalp called "cradle cap" or "cradle crap." Mom says that colic can come from him not having enough of some hormone like "progestrogen" or something. At first he had sticky green poop called "mecomium" or something. Oh my God! Babies are so gross, especially boy babies; I don't want to have any. I hope the next babysitting job I get doesn't include any babies.

In fact, I don't think I ever want babies myself. Especially not BY myself. As mom says, the nuclear family sucks, it's doomed, and single parenting is worse. I would personally like seventeen grandparents, five or six mothers, a few fathers, some sisters and absolutely NO brothers! Nor do I want to spend my whole life moving all over the planet like my mother has. I wish we could just stay in our house forever, but we'll probably have to rent another house in a few months, Mom says. Since Dave left at Christmas, he missed my birthday on December 26th. It really sucks that

it's the day after Christmas, because Mom and my grandparents and everybody says that they'll just combine my
Christmas and birthday gifts. What a rip-off! Right now, on
top of my wish list for birthday gifts would be that my little
brother go to sleep and not wake up again for a long time.
Oh my God! Mom can't even cook supper at night because
she always has her hands full of him screaming. At least
I'm good at Kraft dinner and pork and beans.

We're getting off the ferry now. My mom looks like
she's sleepwalking. And just on the other side of the aisle
is Mr. Wringer and his wife. He's a dentist and my mom is
his hygienist, only she's on maternity leave. She cannot
afford to go back to work, ever, she says, but we're not
supposed to let Mr. Wringer know that or she'll get cut off
her benefits. She says she does most of the icky jobs like
cleaning people's teeth, while he makes most of the
money. Mr. Wringer sees us and waves, but his wife
pretends not to notice us. She's probably in a hurry to get
to the car deck because they announced Horseshoe Bay a
few minutes ago. I notice that Tony lets go of a big fart
and the outside of the Snugli gets all brown and wet. It's
leaking and dripping on the floor and Mom's face is really
red when Mr. Wringer comes over to say hello.

"He's really cute," says Mr. Wringer, but you can tell
he's not even looking at Tony, only at the stain on the
Snugli that's getting bigger and wetter. It really stinks.
His wife says, "Oh, what a little cherub!" as if Tony has
wings sticking out of his Snugli. Instead of looking like

one of the chicks we hatched at school last Easter, all slimy and horrible.

"I guess kids are either the centre of your life or they're not. The rest is just commentary." I am not sure why Mom says this to Mrs. Wringer, but Mrs. Wringer turns bright red. But she must feel real good that at least she doesn't have any kids.

Oh my God! We nearly don't make it off the ferry in time. Mom makes me unpack the small backpack after I get it from the baggage hold so I can get Tony a clean sleeper. Mom says it makes more sense not to get him dressed at all, since he's mostly sleeping or covered up in the Snugli. She says she can't figure out why all her friends give her these cute clothes that he's never going to wear anyway. "Wouldn't you know it?" she says. "I brought lots of diapers and sleepers to change him into, but who'd have thought I'd need another Snugli for the weekend? As if we have two, anyway." Oh great, I think, I have to walk around with Mom all weekend while everybody's staring at her for wearing this brown smelly thing around her neck. We'll have to sit far apart from everyone at the Folk Festival now. I wish I had a magic wand to make him disappear sometimes. Or that we never had to go anywhere and could just stay at home watching TV like most of my friends.

She promised me an ice cream cone for helping her out, and we're catching the city bus that goes through West

Van. There are so many pretty houses and trees through here that I'm enjoying looking out the window. "Wouldn't you love to live here?" I say to her, but she doesn't even look. I brought my pillow with me for the festival and I've been leaning on it against our backpacks, but the sun's getting hot through the window, so I flip the pillow over for the cool side. I'd like to jump into one of those turquoise pools I can see peeking through the trees.

After the whole hassle of changing buses, we get off near Jericho Beach and there's a huge lineup of all kinds of weird people wearing tattoos and stud earrings in their noses and orange and green hairdos. I could look at them all day. They're selling sarongs and T-shirts and earrings and incense and even kites. I wish I could buy some of those things, just to show Lauren when I get back home. But I wouldn't wear stuff like that. Only people my mother's age do. Sometimes she wears these low-cut dresses when she's going out. Like she doesn't realize how horrible it is to show herself off like that. Right now, she's complaining to me about how much getting into the festival costs this year and how she can't believe that it used to be just five dollars a day. She made us pack lunches too, because she said that it would be too expensive to buy our food here. She cooked all kinds of things and froze them before my brother was born so we'd be ready. I've noticed my mom likes to cook a lot when she's upset. So I'm eating my sandwich pretty quick; then I can remind her about my ice cream. Like I would let her forget.

We stand in the lineup for more than an hour and my mom is getting steamed, mostly because Tony's acting up again. It must be the hottest day of the summer. Even my shorts are sticking to me. When we get close enough to the head of the line for me to see the board, there's all these weird flavours I've never heard of before: espresso, venezia, and so on. You'd think they'd have vanilla and chocolate, at least. Mom explains that this is gelati and it's the Italian version of ice cream. Which explains why they charge $5 instead of the usual $2. It's a pretty small ice cream from what I can see and I'm not used to this kind of cone, but I figure I better not make a fuss after we've been waiting that long.

We go to the part of the park where the singer my mom likes is playing. I'm moving too quickly, trying to keep up with her, and of course the stupid gelati falls off the cone and right into the dirt. It makes me cry because I had to wait so long for it and I didn't even get to taste it. Mom says no way are we standing in line again to get another one, which makes me cry even harder. But she just marches straight ahead of me and I know there's no point in arguing with her anymore. By now it's late afternoon and the sun is blistering hot, so I ask her for a drink box from the backpack. It's lemonade, kind of warm and sticky. I wish we could leave here for something really cold. A Coke would be awesome.

That was my favourite part about summer camp the year before last. They had this freezer right outside the kitchen door and whenever you wanted you could take out a freezie all day long. My counsellor never minded how many you had, or whether it would ruin your supper. I nearly never made it to camp at all because my dad had my health record locked up somewhere and I forgot to tell my mom until the Saturday before I was leaving that I had to have it before I could go. Oh my God! At the clinic they tried to look up my record but they couldn't because it was a weekend. My mom was really upset, so we decided to go to the car and sit and think about what to do next. Her period started on the way to the car and would you believe she didn't have any underwear on? It was because she was wearing her old dress that she'd put on early in the morning, meaning to have a shower later. So there we were with two pads in her purse but nothing to stick them onto! Always be prepared, she usually says to me. It was starting to show on the back of her dress but I decided not to bug her about it. Then we realized she'd locked the keys in the car, so we had to walk a mile to the drugstore to buy Tampax while we waited for the locksmith to come. She'd thought we'd only be five minutes at the clinic, so there was the package of hamburger she'd bought for supper at the corner store, leaking all over the car seat. It was a real hot day then, too. Later on that day, Mom called my school secretary who unlocked the school files for us at night, so I got my record in time to catch the bus the next morning. It was a good thing, too. They're very strict about not taking you if you don't have your health card to show.

I'm afraid that if I remind my mom it's nearly supper-time she'll jump all over me. How can she not be hungry after all this time? She's going to listen to some klezmer band now, whatever that is. Of course it has to be way on the other side, just when my arms and back are aching from carrying all this stuff. When we stop, I look hard at my little brother in his blanket. I touch the side of his cheek and he starts turning his head toward my finger. Mom says he's rooting. Makes no sense that he should do things trees are supposed to do. His skin is yellow compared to mine. When we sit down, I play this game with him where I hold a big piece of paper with a bull's eye on it and watch his eyes try to focus. It's hilarious. He makes the sound "ah" over and over again. You'd think he'd get sick of it. Then he tries to hit the paper with his fat little hand. I like to make sounds, like shaking his rattle, and watch him try to figure out where it's coming from. Like I say, babies aren't too smart. At all.

There's this book in the diaper bag Mom carries, called *Infant Colic: What It Is and What You Can Do About It.* What a stupid title! It's written by some doctor, probably a man who never even had a baby. It's pretty obvious even to me that you can't do anything with colicky babies.

I'm not going to be able to stand it much longer. I am so hungry! Can't we eat yet? I ask my mom. "Just wait till this set is over," she whispers. We packed the sandwiches and fruit and drinks in a big cooler yesterday before we left, and of course it's me who has had to lug it around. My stomach is rumbling again. After all the clapping, we finally get up. My leg is all pins and needles. We walk down to the beach, leaving the park, and start in on the sandwiches. They've put up a big wire fence between the beach and the festival so people who haven't paid can't sneak in. When Mom realizes she can hear the music even better just sitting on a beach log, she looks out at the big cargo ships and I see tears all over her face. I sit beside her and put my arms around her; then she looks over and smiles at me. "Sound may travel well, but I sure don't," she says. Whatever.

She makes me find a garbage can for all our stuff while she bundles Tony up. We head to the same bus stop we got off at. I can smell pot everywhere. Mom thinks I don't know what it is, but I have for years. Since grade six, actually, when my friend Crystal brought her boyfriend to the playground after basketball and she asked me did I want to try some? I said no because my Mom was expecting me for supper. This year Crystal started smoking cigarettes too. I'm glad I don't hang out with her anymore. Her mom doesn't even stop her. And for our party last year she wore a low-cut dress and everything, even though nobody else was. Oh my God. What a loser.

I wish my mother wasn't such a space cadet today. She says she understands why having no sleep is used to torture people, that it really works. Even when she has brandy every night, nothing works. It's supposed to go through the same tube as her breast milk and make Tony sleepy, but it doesn't. One time she locked us out of the car two times in one day! The second time, when the same work guy showed up in the parking lot to unlock the car, he had a big grin on his face and she turned beet red. The keys were in the gym bag that she'd put in the trunk, so he had to figure out a way to open the trunk that time. "At least you gave me a challenge this time," he said. It was so totally obvious that he was flirting with her, it just made me sick! Tony was sitting in his car seat in the back of the car, crying away, and all we could do was wave at him through the window and talk baby talk.

Finally we went to Subway for lunch with the money the lady at the gym lent us and he took a long time to get the door open. Tony was bawling away in the back seat the whole time, and Mom was fuming. "It makes me furious that he gives me that look like I'm just another dumb blonde." Which is pretty funny, when you consider that she *is* blonde! "He makes sixty bucks every time I call him. I feel like telling him I'm paying his wages today and he should just shut up." Boy, was she mad! I reminded her that he hadn't said anything mean, but she just stared straight ahead like I wasn't there. And can you believe it? The next time it happened was actually the next week and then she called the only lady locksmith in town because she wasn't going to give that guy the time of day. We made sure to get her business card in case we needed to call her again. Which of course we did. I told my mom that God was trying to tell her something, like maybe she shouldn't go anywhere. She didn't get it. Hardly any adults do. Especially my mother.

She doesn't laugh much anymore. I was kind of hoping this festival would make her a bit happier. It sure is hard to be around her when she's always taking stuff out on me. When she slows down, she says she realizes she'll never be the same age again as she is now and she should enjoy the moment. Whatever. By the time we get to her friend Josh's apartment, which he has lent her for the night since he's away in Toronto, we're both too tired to talk much. After the sandwiches we ate at Jericho for supper, I'm still hungry, so she gives me money to get some chips and stuff at the corner store, and by the time I get back, she looks ready for sleep but of course Tony is practising to be an opera singer again. I wonder how the neighbours in Josh's building are taking this.

That day we went crazy trying to get my medical record for camp she nearly had a nervous breakdown. As soon as she got in the door with her Tampax and said all she wanted was a hot bath, my Aunt Beth called and she was on the phone forever. Later I heard her talking to her friend Suzie about it.

"Beth says to me, after talking for over half an hour, 'Is this a good time to call?' She picks NOW to tell me she's discovered her soul mate and that she might really have been a lesbian all her life and that men's bodies seem hairy and disgusting to her now and will I judge her for this or can she count on my support? All I could think about was how I wanted my bath and how dogshit tired I was, and she thinks that because I don't answer her right away I must be shocked. Why does she have to pick me to tell this to, and why today? Why do I have to be a parent? I want to quit this job. Ten more years of this? God, murderers get shorter sentences." Mom was nearly screaming on the phone at poor Suzie.

It's Sunday and we're going home early. Yesterday was a long day, and I didn't really get into most of the music except for this girl from Nova Scotia. I thought we were going to stay for the whole festival, but I decide I won't ask why we're not. I'm just glad it's over. Mom got really pissed off when she realized that we weren't going to be able to hear much of the music, so she went into this big tent and spent two hundred bucks on CDs and tapes and shoved them into her pack like she was furious with the whole world. Right now the ferry is so crowded and all I want is my own bed and quiet again, if Tony will ever shut up so I can sleep. I doubt it. My life kinda sucks at this point in time.

By the time we get inside the front door, I am ready to collapse. I just drop our bags on the floor, slip my sandals off and head to the bathtub. After a few minutes, Mom comes in and says, "Guess what? The Folk Festival is being recorded live on CBC." She rolls her eyes. She's looking at me with that "you-will-never-understand" face. I get dried off and get into my pajamas slowly, then go to kiss her goodnight and find her asleep beside the stereo speaker. It's the first time I've seen her being still for days. Then Tony wakes up, crying. Oh! My! God!

Wings

I WANNA ORDER ANOTHER BASKET OF WINGS. SO what? I like hot Cajun and I drink hard liquor. Don't you go telling me what's good for me. My ex has been on that one for years and even though this would have been our tenth, he still never managed to get through to me. He'd screw up his face hard and mean and wanna take the whole world out on me. But I got tired of wearing sunglasses all the time, you know what I mean? So I took off fast. Jamie — he's my youngest — only had time to grab his Ninja turtle. He was still wearing his PJs, all soft and sleepy like, but there was no time to pack. I just slipped his little rubber sandals on his feet. Thank Christ the other two were at a sleepover at my girlfriend's place.

Yeah, it's Jacqueline. Not Jackie. I hate that. No, I have an unlisted number.

I know what you're saying. But you can't always be looking into the past all the time. You gotta look out for yourself. No one else will.

So maybe I don't pick 'em so well, but this one owns his own rig and I hate cold sheets. It's got eighteen wheels, bright and shiny like it's always going to stay brand spanking new like that. At least that's what *he* thinks. Me, I get pissed off when he starts telling me not to look at other guys or shoot off my mouth again. And he's got this St. Christopher medal hanging from the rearview. God, I hate having some guy look down on you while you're doing it.

You don't have any heartaches? Well, you musta got lucky is all I can say. Course you're still young yet. I was like you once, willing to give everything. But lately I've lost hope. Though it sure would be nice to have one around on a regular basis. My heart aches. Really it does. Yeah, you're right. It can be real sweet when you're just starting out.

Why is that? At first they say they like you 'cause you're soft and then they set about beating the shit out of the softness. Like you're a pillow made just for their private use or something. I always swore I'd get harder next time. That's what gets me most. They treat you like you're some goddamn canary. They help you grow your wings but no fuckin' way are you supposed to fly.

Anyhow, as I was telling you, then there was this other guy. He was in real estate. Real gentle most of the time. But watch him play baseball and you could guess what you had coming to you if you crossed him. Not that he was ever off the field that long. I just decided not to give it away when it's bloody obvious you're just the filler between stuff that *really* interests them.

One time I was seeing this Nam vet from Brooklyn? But I don't know that he really liked women all that much and I didn't wanna get anything from him. I mean, who knows with this AIDS scare and all. Anyway, all he ever wanted me to do was *talk* and help him out. Christ, I can hardly help myself. I don't mind it when they get all sweaty and raunchy, but who wants to *think* while you're doing it?

Pass down those peanuts. My daughter's always on my case not to eat so much salt. "It'll just get you all bloated again, Mom," she says. As if I didn't know that. I like the taste, I tell her. So what if I *am* putting on a little weight? I tell her I'm going to seed anyway. My reputation's already shot. Not that it was ever all that pure and white to begin with.

Reminds me of when Gina and I made our first communion, all decked out in frilly white dresses exactly the same like we were baby brides or something. Although to tell the truth we looked more like Halloween ghosts, 'cept we had veils and crinolines and bobby socks. Some costumes. We were almost outta the house when she got caught on the fence and it ripped all up one side. The old man started screaming about how we were supposed to *pay attention* and everything, and pretty soon the whole day turned kinda sour. I remember praying real hard in church that day. I made a deal with God that if he let me outta that house alive, I'd even the score some day.

Huh? Yeah, I guess you could say that again. A bully and an asshole to boot. So who has a normal family these days? He was kinda sweet on payday, would buy everyone a round, that's when we knew to ask him for favours we'd saved up all week. I liked him best then. But it only lasted for the first bottle. Then *look out*. Other times he got so wound up he'd have to take his belt to us. I guess I got it worst 'cause I stood up to him and no one else would. Mary Margaret says it's 'cause he loved me most. Funny her being jealous of that all these years.

No. Not any more, anyway. I used to want to make somebody pay, but now I'm just too goddamn tired all the time. Who are you supposed to blame anyway? And you get kinda used to keeping it to yourself 'cause you're the one who knows it best. You know that song by Tom Waits?

Well, the line I like most goes, "If I exorcise my devils, well, my angels may leave too." It's a neat line.

No, thanks. I'm really just playing with these ice cubes, and I don't need another one anyway. You go ahead. I don't mind at all. I'll just finish picking at these bones for a while.

You Are Here

THE GECKOS ARE SCOLDING ALICE AGAIN FROM their perch on the ceiling fan.

The night before, one had dropped onto the bed where she and Gordon lay covered in a wet sheet. They were trying to cool off under the slow, noisy undulations of the fan that churned uselessly through the clammy air, as they battled for sleep. She'd been startled out of a dream in which she'd been sailing on a yacht she'd borrowed from someone, and couldn't remember how to tie a knot at the pier. In the dream, she'd looked around helplessly for someone to assist her, but there was only a little boy fishing on the pier. He paid no attention to her and just smiled. She knew that she would lose the boat, and the friend who had lent it to her, if she did not remember the knot in time. Just when she was on the verge of

teaching her hands to obey her half-remembered instructions — plop — the gecko landed on her shoulder where
she lay curled into Gordon's chest, and she was startled
out of sleep. She tensed her muscles, not remembering
where she was, and then the room became focused again.
In a half-trance, she flicked the gecko off her skin with
one twitch, and then, in a broader and more agitated
sweep, flung it completely off the bed. When she finally
returned to sleep, she dreamed she was being chased by
a giant gecko, and woke up shivering.

Now, in full daylight, the geckos are still chattering on
the ceiling. She hadn't heard them while she and Gordon
were making love last night, but as the two of them lay
back exhausted from their efforts in the heat, she could
hear them saying "tsk tsk" in a monotonous refrain, as if
they disapproved of what they observed below them.
"Listen to them," she said to Gordon. "They sound as
disapproving as your parents." She'd leaned over him,
wagging her index finger and sucking air in between her
teeth in imitation of the clucking geckos until he grinned
up at her. Recalling that now makes her want to tremble
with laughter. Do these ones on the ceiling taunt in Bahasa
Malay, the local dialect, Alice wonders, or is gecko lingo
universal? There is a local mandate that Bahasa Malay be
taught in schools, and used on signs. It reminds her of the
same controversy in Quebec; here the Chinese businesses,
the economic backbone of the country, are pulling up
stakes as rapidly as English businesses in Quebec.

Alice has been feeling rootless, out of place, without direction in a foreign country. She finds herself grateful for her attachment to Gordon, but is still uncertain of her purpose in being here. Maybe it is the final respite before they settle down to the business of raising children. But was this a purpose?

"What do you mean, purpose?" he'd asked her. "Since when do you need a sense of purpose? Just kick back and enjoy the ride."

Gordon has several photography assignments that take him to remoter parts of Malaysia while Alice stays in the larger centres. They've decided to abandon their jobs in Canada to travel together for a year, before they settle down. Gordon thinks of this as a mutual decision, while Alice views it as a compromise.

She pictures herself with no more than two children. She is not sure, though. About anything. She tries to remember why she married him. It would make signing into hotels easier when they travelled, she'd rationalized at the time. They'd already been living together for four months. She'd liked the idea of travelling, but not alone. Alice had been amazed that someone would stay with a woman as complicated as she was. She wanted to be a simpler person, but knew herself incapable of changing.

He has been patient if slightly exasperated with her moodiness of late, not understanding. Nothing was wrong, she'd told him. It's just that nothing was right. Was he strong enough to stick by her even when she said that?

she wondered. Most nights she pleaded with him never to leave her, usually when she was close to orgasm, but she always felt Gordon pulling back into himself only moments after he'd pledged to stay with her forever. Like some amphibious creature, he kept his secrets to himself, neither committing to land nor to water. Meanwhile, as long as he promised he would continue, she believed any comforting lies he offered her.

It is early afternoon now. Alice is lying in bed, fresh from her second shower that day, with a pitcher of lime juice on the bedstand beside her, when she hears the geckos sputtering at her again. She turns her neck upward to scold back at them, and the towel she wears wrapped around her head comes undone. She grabs the towel and begins flinging it at the gecko that is crawling across the wall toward the bed, but it scurries further down the wall and disappears under the crack below the door.

Where is Gordon anyway? She is getting hungry, and he's been gone for hours. All he had to do was change some travellers' cheques before the bank closed. He wanted to change a large amount or he would simply have gone to the Sikh down the street at the bazaar where travellers usually changed money. The same Sikh ran after her every time she left the hotel, yelling, "Memsahib. I can help you with something today? You need trishaw driver? My brother-in-law is famous tour guide. I guarantee you good deal." Gordon had said that he did not want to be a mug with too many bills in his

wallet after changing the cheques. She imagines him
going through the turnstile door at the bank, where a
severe-looking Sikh guards the entrance with a gun that
looked antique — probably a leftover from Dutch East
Indian stock, she fancies. She tries to go back to reading
her book, then gives up and pulls her skirt back on.

In the middle of the heat last night, she and Gordon
had fought. It was probably the heat that made them
wake up in the small hours of the morning; not even
making love, which usually lulled both of them to sleep
most evenings, could guarantee a full night's sleep in
this climate. Alice had brought up the fated question
one more time: when could they have a child? He had
said they could think about it on this trip, but every time
she raised the topic, he was dismissive. Every morning
she dutifully took her birth control pill with her tea, but
fantasized about losing the package and not telling
Gordon. He was evasive when she asked him what his
time frame was. "It will happen in good time," he kept
insisting. But her time was running out. She would be
thirty-four next month.

Alice envies Gordon his assuredness. Gordon had
known he wanted to be a photographer since his grandfather had given him his first camera on his tenth birthday.
He'd studied fine arts at the college where Alice did her
nursing diploma; he'd taken the pictures of the gradu-
ating class of nurses and they'd met over the wine and
cheese reception that followed. Now she has several photo

albums documenting her past year with him. For many years before his appearance in her life, there had been only a handful of pictures of her, and then suddenly he'd made her materialize, brought her an awareness of herself that came from many angles. At first she'd been self-conscious about posing for him, but then gradually became accustomed to his pulling out his camera in mid-conversation and punctuating his speech with pauses during which the flash went off. She hadn't practised nursing more than eight months before she knew she hated it, hated the shift work, hated the brisk impersonality with which she was expected to treat the patients in her care.

"I can never get you just right," he's told her repeatedly. "You're a chameleon, you know."

He still takes many shots of her between his nature assignments for the scientific journals that commission his work. His only disappointment is that he has not sold a picture to *National Geographic*. Not yet, anyway, he often grins. He really believes it is not only possible, but inevitable.

ALICE SCRAWLS A NOTE FOR GORDON, TELLING him to meet her at the restaurant where they ate dinner the night before, and heads down the stairs and out the door to explore their dusty street, Leboh Chulia, for the second time that day. She wades through the humidity that swamps her in waves as she crosses the street.

Alice and Gordon have been staying in Georgetown for more than a week now. Gordon had bartered to get the weekly rate at the Swiss Hotel, which Alice had concluded must be named after the Swiss who built the funicular on Penang Hill that they had ridden several days ago. When that first week was up, the manager called them over to the desk one morning as they were heading out to eat. They realized they'd lost track of time, forgetting that Christmas was only three days away. Holidays had become meaningless on their schedule, since travelling in Southeast Asia for several months meant that every day was a holiday of sorts, something that had taken Alice several weeks to adjust to at the onset of their journey. They'd wanted to keep their hotel room here, dreading the idea of travel over the holidays. The Chinese hotel manager held up the calendar that advertised Danish Butter Cookies amidst the demented grins of blond Western children, a boy and a girl with far-set eyes, and made it clear to them that the room would now cost double because of the approaching holidays. Alice and Gordon had shrugged their shoulders helplessly and then went out to have a cold Singha beer. It had been too hot to argue.

Georgetown, sleep or no sleep, delights her. The back alleys are better, somehow more Chinese than those in Hong Kong, where she and Gordon had had a dreadful and expensive holiday after the photography assignment in Taipei. She loves the old grandmothers, whose energetic cackling around the food stalls is enthralling. They parade young children with shiny faces and new hats to all the foreigners, and then huddle around them protectively. Riding the trishaws at night, when there is less dust, gazing at all the stalls lit up like Christmas and hearing the continuous clack of mah-jong tiles that travels the air from the open windows of houses like exotic castanets, she feels that the town has an aura of magic. In the daytime, Alice loves the trilling of caged songbirds that reaches her ears from the same open windows, but by day, the mah-jong tiles sound more like a mild game of marbles. She watches the Tamil Indians cooling hot milk by tossing it from one cup to another. She has spent many melancholy hours wandering around the graveyard at the Cathedral of the Assumption, admiring its double spires, reading the wistful stories of homesick English administrators and their families carved on tombstones. Below the tombs are the ancestral bones of the Malays who had been converted by successive waves of missionaries, the guide, a student with broken teeth and radical politics, explained to her. History buried in layers. How like the natives in Canada, thinks Alice. Why does she keep thinking about home? Why can't she just be here, as everyone else seems to be?

In the restaurant, Chinese dragons chase each other across the wall, and joss sticks smoke below the shrine to the owner's ancestors, whose pictures are framed behind glass clouded with moisture; the menu features

Chinese and Indian food. Last night Gordon had ordered a large plate of curried chicken called Curry Kapitan, which a traveller from Belgium had told them was named after a Dutch sea captain who asked his mess boy what was for dinner, to which he received the reply, "Curry, kapitan." Was this just apocryphal? Or a racist joke? Alice has no way of knowing the truth about anything here.

Nearing the restaurant again, Alice slows her pace after her short, brisk walk through the streets. She sees Gordon go in ahead of her; he has come from the other side of the entrance and does not notice her. Good, that means he got her note. When she passes through the beaded entranceway, she recognizes the Aussie seated at the table ahead of her as the same one she had met several days ago, outside the entrance to the Kapitan Kling mosque, a yellow building with a single minaret. His towering build and reddish blond hair had struck Alice immediately; next to the squat Indians leaving the mosque, he seemed like the Jolly Green Giant. They had spoken briefly in front of the sign that spelled out, in the flawed English that characterized similar signs, the list of rules for female tourists entering mosques:

WOMEN MUST WHERE MODEST CLOTHS.
NO EXPOSED SHOULDERS.
NO NECKLINES TOO LOW.
NO SHORTS SKIRTS.
REMOVE ALL SANDALS.

This time the Giant introduces himself as Brad, and gestures toward the fellow seated beside him with his thumb: "This is Calvin," he mumbles, his mouth full, "Med student from Kent." "And I am Marie-Louise," adds the petite French woman across the table, her face turned up to Gordon. Wings of soft brunette hair frame her face. Alice had already met Marie-Louise last week, but Gordon has not met her yet. Brad had been the one to tell Gordon and Alice to go and see the wonderful waterfall the day they had met at the mosque. Alice had taken his advice and had enjoyed all the chattering monkeys while Gordon had read the newspaper in the shade. Now Alice waves to Gordon, who holds up a fistful of bills to indicate he's had success in cashing the traveller's cheques. Alice is about to introduce herself to Brad's companions in turn, when her voice is drowned out by a Chinese funeral procession wailing through the streets. They all raise their fingers to plug their ears.

"Sounds like a bloody Dixieland band," moans Brad.

"Yeah, between that and the call to prayer at all hours of the day, it's a wonder anyone in this town can sleep at all," adds Calvin.

"Did anyone else hear that truck come by with the megaphone in the middle of the night? Is it election time or what?" Brad inquires. Alice sits down, defeated by the noise. She can't add much to the conversation. "Wait till you hear what happened at the bloody bank," says Gordon, rolling his eyes. Clearly he doesn't want to tell the story right now, as he turns his attention to the menu. Alice gives the waiter her order, listening half-heartedly to the others discussing varieties of beer and favourite beaches. The men agree that the north coast of Penang has the best sand beaches for foreigners to enjoy, locally called *batu ferringhi* or "foreigners' beaches." Hearing this, Alice explains why she refuses to suntan on the beach anymore.

"All these kids kept chasing me, waiting to see where I would put my towel down. Then they would want a photo with me. 'Photo, please lady!'" she mimics in a high voice. Her food arrives and she is momentarily interrupted.

"I guess the idea of trying to darken your skin is bizarre to them. Only peasants who have to work in the sun have dark skin. And the women in the countryside cover themselves from head to toe, while there I was roasting myself like something on a barbecue. I couldn't stand getting hassled anymore. I felt ridiculous." Already Alice's tan has started to fade. She wears her Chinese straw coolie hat more often when she goes out, the one she bought at the old fishing village near the ferry terminal where they had landed when they came over from Butterworth. Alice remembers the day that she purchased it, and the haggling she had done to lower the price.

"Imagine, we will have suntans and sunshine and no snow for Christmas. But of course, you are used to that." Marie-Louise looks with tenderness at the Aussie, who shrugs his shoulders and says, "Yeah, well, Christmas never meant all that much to me anyway. At least most of the restaurants around here won't be shut," he snorted.

Alice is not surprised by Brad's comment, only saddened. Her memories of Christmas are robust and cheerful: she remembers her brother and sisters dressed in the plaid vests and skirts that her mother favoured for the holiday season, dazzling tree lights, the scent of cinnamon from the apple cider brewing in the kitchen, well-lit parks, the windows at Eaton's decorated with animals from the North Pole that hammered and skated in time to the music. In all the snapshots of her childhood, Alice and her siblings glow with goodwill at Christmas, opening presents graciously, perhaps only for that one time of the year sharing their toys. She is surprised only by the sudden wave of nostalgia she feels now.

Alice is also surprised at her own easy acceptance of Marie-Louise's state, how unwittingly she's invited Marie-Louise's confidence. When the French woman had rapped on her door last week, Alice had been astonished at the presumptuous manner in which Marie-Louise flung herself down on the bed where Gordon's clothes lay fresh from the clothesline. They had only met the day before and spoken briefly on the rooftop, where they were hanging out clothes and sharing the same wash-bucket full of clothespins. But on that day Marie-Louise spoke to her as if they had been longtime friends.

"My boyfriend will kill me," sputtered Marie-Louise, hugging the pillow to her stomach. "There is no way to tell him. Mon Dieu, what shall I do?" Alice assumed she meant her boyfriend in France, but didn't want to inquire. Was she pregnant just before she left? Yesterday she had told Alice she had been in Malaysia for only a few weeks, and that she wasn't sure how things stood with her lover in France.

It had taken Alice nearly an hour to calm Marie-Louise down and to make her stop crying long enough to consider what alternatives, if any, might be available to a pregnant woman in Malaysia. Not exactly the kind of information listed in her travel guide. "Get a grip," she'd wanted to say, but refrained, inwardly chastising herself for her lack of compassion. Why are the French always so melodramatic, and why do they take so long to get to the point? She had found herself wondering why she wanted to make these generalizations. But then, Alice reflected, when she was with British people, she found herself frustrated at their inability to be demonstrative, their cut-and-dried approach to everything. An unfortunate expression, that, given that Marie-Louise was wailing that she had never had an abortion before and wasn't at all sure she could go through with it.

"Will you help me, Aleece?" Marie-Louise had asked, her upturned chin dripping with tears.

"Of course I will. But I'm not at all sure what I can do."

"And please, tell no one."

"I won't. Do you have enough money, if there is a clinic in K.L.?" Alice had already adopted the local practice of referring to the capital by its initials.

"I think yes. It will mean I must return early to France, but perhaps that is the best."

Alice had felt relieved when Marie-Louise finally left the room. She hadn't sought Alice out afterward, and several days had passed. Alice told herself that she was respecting Marie-Louise's privacy, that she didn't want to embarrass her while others were around by suggesting a girls' talk. Alice hadn't even confided in Gordon, although she usually told him things that others had made her swear never to reveal. She hadn't even introduced her to him. She wasn't entirely sure why she was hanging on to the secret. Maybe she really did like Marie-Louise, wanted to protect her?

"How about meeting on that hotel balcony. What's it called?" Calvin says.

"The Eng Aun. It's across from our hotel," replies Alice, grateful that her mind hasn't completely wandered away and she has something to contribute to this conversation. "They make great breakfast omelettes."

When Brad, Calvin, Alice and Gordon convene on the balcony at breakfast the next morning, they are grateful for its coolness. The day promises to be another scorcher already. The wrought-iron railings afford an unobstructed view of the street below, where Alice glimpses the familiar tie-dye purple of Marie-Louise's sarong as she crosses in front of a bicycle, sending its rider careening into the middle lane and cursing.

"Are you okay?" Alice leans over the balustrade and calls out instinctively. Marie-Louise should have crossed at the intersection. Any sensible person would know that this morning traffic is murder, thinks Alice. Marie-Louise skips up the steps to the Eng Aun Hotel and disappears into the shadows before re-emerging on the balcony minutes later, accompanied by the waiter. She spreads her sarong demurely over the chair she pulls up and orders toast from the young Chinese boy.

"Really, we should do something to celebrate Christmas," protests Calvin to Brad, who has been mocking the Chinese Santa Claus on the street below them. Calvin removes his glasses and wipes the steam from them on his T-shirt. Gordon is silent. He wakes up slowly in the mornings, and the instant Nescafé is weaker than usual here. The waiter returns and sets a plate of toast and a cup of tea in front of Marie-Louise.

"I reckon a good piss-up would be just the ticket then," says Brad.

"But, Bradley," protests Marie-Louise, "it must be a real meal, with the little hors d'oeuvres, some good wine if we can find this, maybe a fine bread, not this sheet with too much sugar." She gestures toward the toast on the plate in front of her. Ants are crawling up the side of the jam jar beside the plate. Seeing the plate, Alice regrets ordering toast.

"Well, then, right-o. Me and my mate will see what we can conjure up. But right now we're off to see the reclining Buddha." Brad rises to his feet and stretches his arms above his head, so that the hem of his T-shirt rides above his belted jeans and furry belly button. Calvin stands up after him, muttering something about finding his sunglasses and camera before they leave.

"The guy at the gate will try to tell you that it's the longest Buddha in the world," Alice throws in as the two men depart for their rooms. "But it's really only 32 metres. Anyway, I'm sure that Buddha in Bangkok — what was it called, Gordon? — must be much longer."

"They bloody well all want to be the longest," retorts Brad as he closes the screen door to the balcony behind him. Marie-Louise makes a neat pile of toast crumbs on her plate, using her thumb and index finger, then lifts her magazine up and slips her marmalade jar into the crook of her arm as she leaves the verandah.

"See you later," she murmurs softly to Gordon and Alice. Her voice is not strong.

The day is already too warm to venture out, so Gordon and Alice retreat to their hotel room across the road. Alice's shirt is drenched under the arms and near the waist where it is tucked into her skirt.

⁀

"IT'S ALREADY THE DAY BEFORE CHRISTMAS," announces Gordon to Alice the next day, as they walk

to the café that specializes in murtabak, a place they
return to often for lunch because they're unable to resist
the smell from the open griddle on the street.

She's grown accustomed to washing her hands in the
sink provided at the back of Indian restaurants, and
pretending that she has no left hand as she scoops up her
food with her roti. The left hand is only to be used in
the toilet, she'd been reminded over and over by Gordon
before they had come to Malaysia. She watches the
Muslim pour a sizzling egg mixture filled with vegeta-
bles and lamb on the griddle outside the restaurant, then
stuff it into a thin roti pastry that he carries ceremoniously inside and sets down on a table, a glass of lime
juice beside it to wash down her meal. It's while she
glances at her face in the mirror above the sink that she
catches sight of Calvin, Brad and Marie-Louise in a dark,
smoky corner of the restaurant. All the Westerners in
town seem to patronize the same three restaurants. She
signals Gordon, points to the corner, then saunters over
to their table, pulling over a chair with her. Gordon finds
a chair from the other side of the restaurant and joins
them. The waiter sighs and moves their plates over to
the larger table. Marie-Louise gazes longingly at Brad,
while Calvin consults his travel guide at random, flipping
the pages. They seem to welcome her joining them,
making too much of a fuss and dragging the table beside
them over to connect with theirs. Alice feels she has
disturbed some drama; clearly they've been discussing

something that has left them awkward and eager for distraction.

"So, have you figured out what we're doing for the feast of our Lord's birth?" intones Calvin, his voice mocking and his eyes twinkling.

"I was just going to ask you the same thing," says Alice. Another plate of murtabak is set down on the table, and Gordon walks toward them from the direction of the sink, where he's washed his hands after ordering. "Obviously the reclining Buddha didn't inspire you enormously. Were you underimpressed?"

"It was all right," admits Calvin. "They all start to look alike after a while. But what about what we're going to do for this holiday thing?"

"How about some Christmas cheer?" asks Gordon. "Something a little stronger than beer, anyway."

"Seems like we're on the same wavelength," exclaims Brad. Alice tears into her roti and nods enthusiastically. She swallows, takes a gulp of lime juice, and then asks who wants to go shopping after lunch; only one more could fit in a trishaw with her. Marie-Louise turns her head and stares out the window.

"I need to catch a nap and then post a few letters," mutters Calvin.

"I'll volunteer," says Brad. He's shredding the napkin into thin strips on top of his empty plate.

"As soon as I'm done eating, shall we head off then?" asks Alice.

"Suits me fine."

"I was also thinking," she says, between mouthfuls, "that maybe we could all buy small gifts — you know, buy one each, then pull names from a hat, that sort of thing."

"Fine by me," concedes Calvin. Marie-Louise continues to ignore them, staring ahead, moody. Calvin slams the book shut and stands, his exposed flesh below his walking shorts making a ripping noise as it peels off the chair.

Alice hurriedly eats the remainder of her murtabak, uncertain if she had interrupted a scene when she and Gordon had seated themselves at the table. Gordon and Brad chat together, but she can't make out what they're saying. Finally she wipes her plate with the last of the roti and stands up, her hand on Gordon's shoulder. He slings his camera over his other shoulder, and then turns to speak to her.

"Catch you later then, love. Buy me something nice." She aims to give Gordon a quick kiss on the cheek, but misses, and her lips encounter his beard. By the time she adjusts her handbag and finds her straw hat, Brad is already waiting on the street, searching for a trishaw driver, his arm raised high in the air. The trishaw driver is likely in his twenties, but his face is riddled with acne scars and his teeth are rotting, making him appear much older. He scowls when Brad says they are looking for the English grocery called Cold Store.

"Cold Storage Supermarket, sir?"

"Yeah, that's what it's called," replies Brad. The driver had obviously been hoping for a more lucrative fare, but he pinches his lips together soberly and turns the cart back into the traffic.

"How did you hear about this place?" asked Alice.

"Some fellow frog told Marie-Louise," he replies. Alice winces at the term "frog," but decides not to make an issue of it. Brad is a large man who takes up most of the seat in the trishaw, and she senses that he could use his size to intimidate those who oppose him. Feeling squished already, she tries a lighter note.

"Do I take it that you're not too fond of the French, then?"

"It's just her," he grimaces. "Can't seem to shake her. I'm not ready to head back to Singapore yet, but I bloody well may have to, if she doesn't get off my case."

"It's obvious she's drawn to you right now," says Alice. She can't tell him about Marie-Louise's condition. But she wishes she could ask him to be a little more understanding. Brad offers no reply, but grips the side of the cart as if he were pumping the metal. Obviously not something he wants to talk about, thinks Alice, so she tries changing the topic.

"I thought we might try checking out the market stalls if we don't find anything here. I wanted to find some treats so we could just snack and drink tomorrow night, so I'm hoping this shop has good stuff. God, what I wouldn't give for some chocolate!" she prattles on nervously. It's then that she notices Brad's large hand on her thigh. "Some really good chocolate, of course, Belgian or Swiss," she adds, moving her leg away. Brad seems to relax, shifting his weight to the other side of the seat. "I can't bear that waxy American stuff," she continues, determined to conquer the silence.

The trishaw driver comes to a screeching halt that throws both Brad and Alice forward. She reaches for her wallet to pay him, but Brad already has his money out. When they step down, Alice offers him some coins, but he brushes her away and moves swiftly toward the Cold Storage Supermarket. After half an hour, exclaiming delightedly at their discoveries, they settle on some Stilton that, though mouldy, reminds them both of home and how long it has been since they've eaten cheese. It's outrageously priced, especially given that it will be reduced to half its size after the mould's cut off. High on a shelf they find a dusty bottle of Courvoisier, its label torn and frayed at the edges. Miraculously its contents are unevaporated. Brad and Alice smile broadly at each other as they both reach for it.

From the supermarket, they head toward the market, where they separate briefly. Alice chooses brightly coloured butterfly hair clips for Marie-Louise, and blank hardcover books covered in bold red Chinese pagodas for Brad and Calvin. For Gordon, she buys boxer shorts with an Oriental-looking Santa Claus smiling across the crotch and demented reindeer trailing across the cuffs.

Feeling dizzy and lightheaded, she stops at a stall for what the vendor assures her is medicinal tea. The sign reads: "Good for cholera, headache, gas, all ills." Good for everything, obviously, even if you don't know what you have, she thinks. Feeling delighted with herself for seeing them out of the corner of her eye, Alice buys a string of tiny Christmas lights, only a third of its lights missing; buried under them is a box of faded Christmas crackers and Santa party hats that read "Mary Christmas." Finally she finds half a dozen shot glasses at the stall that sells kitchen trinkets. When she meets Brad at the kiosk near the entrance to the market, Alice feels exhausted.

"I do believe it's time for afternoon cocktails," she says to him, feigning an English accent.

"Quite," he replies. "Do let me escort Madame home." He bows and signals for a trishaw. Any discomfort Alice had sensed between them earlier seems to have evaporated in the afternoon humidity.

Christmas Day arrives with the same dusty fanfare on the street as any other day, but Alice can barely restrain her excitement as she wraps her small presents in tissue paper. She has a shower late in the afternoon after writing long letters to her sisters and brother back home. At dusk, she arranges the lights on the veranda of the Swiss Hotel; the proprietor has agreed to let her use the extension cord that was usually attached to the neon hotel sign only for the one night because he understood that "is Chrisymass." She sets paper hats and Christmas crackers beside each of the shot glasses she arranges on the tables. Alice also sets the hotel's portable radio that normally sits at the reception desk out on the deck, a privilege she earned by promising the old clerk a drink later that night. She turns the dial to BBC, and the clarion voices of a boys' choir singing "It Came Upon a Midnight Clear" reverberate across the concrete porch. Brad has his feet perched on a chair and is cradling a beer bottle in his lap. He had offered to help Alice, more out of courtesy than genuine desire, she surmises, but she told him to relax. And, in truth, she is enjoying herself.

When they open the Courvoisier and toast each other's health numerous times, a warmth opens in Alice's chest that is surely not just due to the alcohol. She looks about her and feels a genuine fondness for the doddering old desk clerk, who dozes in a chair near the door, the plastic fly strips feathering against his arm in the evening breeze. Her gift from Marie-Louise, a batik pillowslip in vibrant fuchsia, lies neatly folded on the table in front of her, glowing in the candlelight, where its colours remind Alice of a sunset. They trade Christmas stories, regale each other with accounts of their worst meals ever and their most catastrophic travel tales. Gordon is expansive, telling his favourite bear story from when he photographed grizzlies in the Yukon one summer. Alice has heard the story before, and admires the way he tells it. Brad has given her a bag of granola he found at the Cold Storage Supermarket. "Sorry, no chocolate," he adds.

And Calvin had found a sci-fi thriller for Gordon and Alice called *Tales from Another World* at the used-book market stall. She is pleased at the camaraderie, at the soothing ambience that's settled upon all of them as gently as the breeze that flutters across the balcony, carrying mixed smells of fish and dust. Acting on impulse, Marie-Louise persuades them to sign their names and addresses in the Chinese books Alice bought for Calvin and Brad, and to swear that they will write to each other each Christmas from then on. Drunkenly, they all agree it is a good idea. It is well after midnight when they finish singing one more version of "We Three Kings," startling the manager awake by arguing over the lyrics to the final verse. Finally they make up their own version, which they swear they will commit to memory; it is full of vulgar rhymes that are unforgettably rude.

IT IS TRUE THAT MOST OF THEM WILL NOT remember this final verse. They will forget names and faces and voices. Things will pass. The batik pillowcase will leave dye stains all over Alice's pillow and will be consigned to the rag pile in the basement within four months of Alice arriving back in Canada. She will come across it when dusting out the furnace vents over a year later and her heart will lurch as she remembers the hangover she had the morning after Christmas. She had been munching on the granola in bed before falling asleep and left the bag open. In the morning, she had been greeted by a gecko's startled face when, turning the pages of her book, *Tales from Another World*, she absentmind-edly stuck her hand in the bag. Her startled cry almost chased away the wicked hangover. Alice will write to Marie-Louise for two years at Christmas, but never respond to the heart-wrenching letter in which Marie-Louise reveals that a botched abortion has rendered her infertile, that Brad had fathered the child, but that he knew nothing of it. Alice will not know what to write in return that doesn't sound trite or conventionally sympa-thetic. She will think of writing Brad when her divorce with Gordon is final, but by then she will have lost his address. Nor could she have known that he and Calvin would be happily coupled and living in San Francisco, and that his old address was abandoned long ago.

But this is also true: every now and then, at Christmas-time, in one city or another, in high-rises, or suburban split levels, in expensive but unsatisfactory rented rooms with too much forced-air heating, when unconsoling arms turn away from them at night, when the rush of a deep suburban silence engulfs them after a dinner of too much turkey, when indigestion and too much liquor make them roll over in bed with a groan, they will each dream of the midnight breeze that swept across the strait in Malaysia one Christmas Day earlier in their lives.

A warm breeze that fuelled their appetites, fed their separate and undisclosed dreams. They will remember a meal that made no ethnic sense, and songs that had no distinct words. They will remember that they were merry.

TSK. TSK. STAY PRESENT, ALICE SAYS TO HERSELF. She has taken to scolding herself the way the geckos scold at her. She pinches herself, and reminds herself that this is Christmas and that this is her life. This is Christmas Eve, she corrects herself. You are in Georgetown. You do not know where your life will lead you. You are here, she says to herself. You are here.

Deflection

LIGHT WAVES TRAVEL IN A STRAIGHT LINE UNTIL
they encounter a barrier, in which case they slow down
and shift direction. Anyone knows this, Marcy says aloud,
uncorking the Pinot Noir. Maybe all energy works that
way, she muses. She will pour herself a glass now, so that
it will have had time to breathe while she finishes the
vacuuming. A little treat to get through the dreaded task.

Marcy would like to meet her husband's first wife,
she thinks. Not before, but now. Now that her marriage
has been asphyxiated. She heard the death rattle one day
when she turned on the vacuum cleaner in the kids'
room; the clanking hung in her ears forever. It was rather
like when one of the kids had turned down the volume
on the phone so she could only hear a dim reverberation
at first. Marcy was not sure. Some vital Lego parts, no

doubt, sucked up into hollow metal. If her son were not such a little god, she would hide every piece of Lego she found in the house. But the little thief would probably just "borrow" more from his friends. He was too cute for his own good.

Marcy's husband would never tell her why his first marriage ended. All he would say is that Laura left him and came back to Vancouver, where they had started their journey, before they began managing a banana plantation in Israel. That he went off to Paris with a young graphic designer to console himself for a few months, farmed in P.E.I. for a year after he tired of the distracting affair and eventually worked his way back to the West Coast. There he met Laura again in a small restaurant, now unrecognizably trendy. Her skin was orange from eating nothing but carrots, he said; her hair dyed black. It was something to do with poor communication.

The phone really does ring now. Just when Marcy is sitting down to a glass of red wine. It's her Aunt Else. Else rarely calls anymore. Not that she doesn't care about Marcy, it's just that most of the people who are old enough to really interest her are dead. Marcy listens, entranced by the cadence of Else's voice; her ears are still resonating, so at first she doesn't really hear what Else says, this matriarch who married a piano tuner, who switched countries, whose apple cake makes Marcy weak in the knees. "They're sending the electrician over to fix it," Else continues, "but I have no power until this afternoon and Sara is coming for lunch. What will I do?"

Marcy's uncle died at seventy-nine and left Else alone
with all his tuning instruments. Else wept for nearly a
year after he passed away, the clear notes struck by his
tuning fork carving out a path of sound that still rings
out memories. Now she sings to Marcy on the phone in
all the lilts and slurs of a rural Danish accent. She has
probably called to say that her elder sister is in the
hospital, not knowing that Marcy has already heard the
news. But it is unwise to guess why any member of
Marcy's family has called. Else mentions the name of the
hospital second, so that is likely the important thing. If
it were something really important, she would slip it in
sideways, just before the end of the call. Most likely she
has forgotten why she called; perhaps to warn Marcy
that Else is the oldest link in her lineage, and that after
she dies Marcy will be alone with her vacuum cleaner
and her red wine.

Her voice brings to mind the chorus of Marcy's family
gathered. Year after year, descant and chorus. Uncle
Heine, standing on the chair at Christmas, leading the
hymns and compelling everyone's laughter. Flapping his
arms in the air like some demented conductor of musical
souls, a stork unable to extend its wings for all the
surrounding relatives. His wife Maren, embarrassed by
his frivolity, rearranging the food on the table, lighting
the Jule candles. Children, stealing pre-dinner cookies
from the stove, bounce off Great-Uncle Bent, who is

making his way to the back room to have a drink with all the male relations, avoiding the hematite eye of Marcy's grandmother. Marcy's cousin Pia, who cannot even say "hello" without employing an entire major scale, her giggles spreading ripples in the air. And Uncle Bjerne, stern and unrelenting in his admonition to tone it down.

When Marcy asked her husband for more details about Laura and their long marriage, he grew as silent as the obsidian that formed the centre of his rock collection on the mantelpiece. Marcy's husband inspects rocks for a living; they occupied a huge area of their home before he left. When she dusted them, she pondered how rocks resist force, but wear down slowly. Made of fine silt grown hard over time, she once considered rocks constant, patient and immutable. Before, it seemed to her that rocks had no home until you put them in your pocket, one at a time. A few years after she married her husband, Marcy had found a photograph of Laura between the pages of a book. Laura had Pre-Raphaelite hair, luminous skin and a twelve-stringed, long-necked guitar. "Yes, she was a folksinger," he had finally conceded. "She had the voice of an angel." After the divorce in Vancouver, she moved to England, married a minister, and now he has heard that she spends her days lighting candles in a church. Marcy pictures the waves of wax forming dark puddles, the gentle flickering of votive lights.

After she hangs up the phone, Marcy returns the vacuum cleaner to the linen closet and picks up her glass of wine slowly before taking a sip. Then she sets leftover meatloaf on the table and eats it, cold, under the glare of the fluorescent kitchen light. When she finishes scraping her plate, she pours herself another glass of wine, puts on her sandals and heads out to the garden. Near the sandbox Marcy nearly trips over a tiny rock hammer, a gift to her son from his father. It looks oddly like a tool of divination resting on the altar of the wooden sandbox and glinting in the sun. She remembers her son's fierce smashing of a conglomerate rock last week, how he watched delightedly as the pieces bounded off in every direction. Marcy has been told that this is a good thing, that it exposes mystery, gives us stories about the formation of the earth. As her son discovered, it may be true that rocks only betray, topple over, when one tries to build something with them.

Marcy inhales crisp autumn air deeply. Nearly dusk. Along the horizon the sun flickers pinkly on the grey mountain range, not quite extinguished. She walks along the ground and listens to the whisper of leaves as they rustle against her feet. When the wind picks up in an hour, it will whistle and flutter through the apple tree, a whirling vortex through dead leaves on the lawn. Marcy exhales. Thinks of all the excavations to be undertaken. Layers of history to be unearthed and analyzed, then catalogued. Wanting her errors to be contained in the fluid readiness of molten lava, singing into the singe of hot ash and rubble.

Marcy reminds herself that, if she doesn't hear from Aunt Else again soon, she'll have to visit her. Marcy has been thinking of doing something with her hair. She wonders if Else will like it dyed red.

Sunday

PATRICIA HAD COME INTO THE OFFICE ON FRIDAY, limping. It was difficult to meet her boss's eye when he stared quizzically at her, but his square-jawed face wore an expression that clearly demanded a response. "Playmobil," she sputtered. "My son left all the Playmobil pieces on the kitchen floor and I slid on one in the middle of the night when I got up to get a drink of water." Vern rolled his eyes in exasperation. At what? thought Patricia. At her stupidity? How could a man who had never raised small children possibly understand? Maybe he's never heard of Playmobil, that's it. He doesn't know what I'm talking about. She noted that he was wearing his red-striped tie. She's developed a game with herself: she tries to determine if there is a predictable pattern between Vern's choice in ties and his mood swings. Not that he

would ever admit to having mood swings, or even moods.
Vern was fond of using terms like "the bottom line" and
often called her on Sunday afternoons to ask her to
prepare backgrounds for their breakfast meetings.

Patricia wonders, not for the first time, if she should
have accepted the ADM position when it was offered to
her three years ago at Thanksgiving. She often thinks Vern
should be the assistant, and she should be the Deputy
Minister of Health, given his lack of organizational skills.
On bad days, she feels like an overpaid secretary — or not
paid at all, since he simply expects her to be "on the ball"
and compliments her on looking so "bright-eyed and
bushy-tailed," without reference to her solid policy work.

Vern had let her postpone the acceptance of the job
for a month when he heard about Zachary's birth. He
had asked her to apply for it when she was on the
Hospital Research and Development Committee with
him, told Patricia he'd been impressed with her handling
of the presentation to the Board and thought she could
take on a bigger portfolio. Vern had been solicitous and
gallant throughout Patricia's pregnancy, but he made it
clear that he expected she was not the kind of woman
who'd stay home longer than six weeks to "recover from
the birth ordeal." He'd had his secretary send real orchids
to her room at the hospital with a note in his familiar
report handwriting: "Congratulations on your healthy
baby boy." All this was before anyone knew about
Zachary. Including Patricia.

She hadn't quite believed it at first. Standing beside his incubator, staring at the small shaven head with tubes emerging from it in — count them — one, two, three, four, no, five directions, Patricia could scarcely comprehend that this was her son. Perhaps there was some mistake; the "Do Not Resuscitate" sign belonged on another couple's baby, not the child that she and Ron had dreamed about for the past year. For several days, after watching the tiny creature wracked by seizure after seizure, she actually prayed that he might die. Then she would feel guilty for such thoughts, and even guiltier for her lack of connection with the small, spindly being whose snatches of laboured breathing made her feel sick in the pit of her stomach. Her breast milk had leaked all over the blue hospital gown, leaving it so stiff when it dried that she had to change every two hours. When she pumped her milk and flushed it down the bathroom sink, she shook with fury. Only to have to do it all over again, a couple of hours later, her nipples as tight as if caught in a vise. That Zack had pulled through those early weeks was a tribute to his perseverance, and a constant reminder to Patricia that she'd lacked the requisite faith.

She made up for it now. Learned all the buzzwords. Sat on a committee for the rights of the disabled. Studied all the medical literature on his condition, visited with and questioned various homecare workers, pediatricians and physiotherapists. When Zachary was able to sit, with some assistance, at three years old, she was elated,

proud of the exercises she and Ron had dutifully practised with their son every night. Even though Zack
usually just flopped over on his side and blew spit
bubbles at them. He was the physical size of an eighteen-
month-old baby. She loved his drooling smile, his dumb,
lopsided grin. She could nearly forgive herself for having
wished Zachary were someone else rather than their son
for the first year of his life, unable to accept that someone
so imperfect had come from her own body. Daily, Zachary
reminded her that she had no control, that he was ten
times bigger than she was. He will never walk, never talk.
But he will loom over her more powerfully than God.

.⤳

PATRICIA POURS HERSELF A MUG OF COFFEE FROM
the morning's pot on the stove. She takes the carton of
cream — her only luxury — from the fridge, and drib-
bles it into the mug, watching the clouds swirl around
and around before setting it on the microwave tray and
pressing the Beverage button. Tomorrow is Monday. She
will need to arrive half an hour early to complete the
report that was due on Friday afternoon. Must call FedEx
before leaving the house, so it gets delivered on time.
Trash day, too. Did Ron find the lid to the trashcan after
it blew away in the storm last week? And Max's birthday.
She'd committed herself to twenty-nine rice crispy
squares — that's twenty-eight for his classmates and one
for the birthday boy, the teacher had reminded her when

she'd picked him up last week. Not his favourite, but they require no baking. She'll make them after the kids are in bed. Are there any marshmallows left? The corner store is only open until eight. Really, all that's left on that report is tightening up the conclusion. There goes the microwave beep. Who was it she was supposed to contact about the meeting next Thursday? Did Hanna say she was free for lunch this Wednesday, or was it the next one they made arrangements for? Must check her dayplanner.

Zachary's wail crescendos as his spasms increase. It's 7:15, so it's two and a quarter hours since his last meds, and that was 10 ccs, so maybe if she gives him 15 ccs this time, he'll calm down by the time Max gets to sleep. Patricia goes to the kitchen cupboard above the cutlery drawer and takes out the syringe and bottle. She sticks the needle through the rubber stopper and slides the plunger back, then moves toward Zachary's room. When she was carrying Zachary, she had dreamed of reading to both children together at night, of leaving the light on just a little longer so that Max could teach his younger sibling to sound out the words. She would feel that warm glow of love as she listened approvingly from the kitchen, where she loaded the dishwasher. The only warm glow she felt these days was at the centre of her belly, and it had more to do with rage. Where to send it, that rage?

She'd tucked Max in tonight and wondered if she shouldn't be spending more time with him. He seemed stuck in some time warp where he repeated the same expressions as endlessly as he set up his wooden train tracks and sent the railcars round and round the figure-eight track. "You're an anus," he giggled gleefully as she pulled the cover over him. "OOPS, I mean, that's Uranus," he added, pointing shakily to his ceiling at the planet stickers that glowed in the dark. He had tried the same joke on her for at least a week running, but it still made him hysterical.

Patricia needs coffee to keep going. She should go reheat the coffee in the microwave; it's probably cold by now. It is true that she could have quit the Ministry altogether. Ron had reminded her that this was a possibility when she had raised the question late one night. He had held her tight against his chest as her tears spilled all over the T-shirt and boxers he wore to bed. Max was sleeping soundly under his ceiling of glowing stars and planets, so it was all right. Having slept naked all their married life, Patricia and Ron had taken to wearing their underclothes or gym clothes to bed because they had to take turns sitting up with Zack throughout the night. They rarely made love now, but there was tenderness in the way they held hands that had not existed before. Pre-Zack. They had also once slept for deliciously long periods, uninterrupted, told each other their dreams upon waking. Pre Zack.

Heather and Bob had been over last weekend. A rare occurrence, to see them both together. Bob was a physician and Heather always claimed that she was the midwife to their four kids. She'd completed a music degree, and told her friends that she could always return to the cello after the kids were all in school; it wasn't as if she was missing anything. Heather and Patricia had met in Biology 210 back in 1979, and Heather had maintained the contact. For this, Patricia was grateful and mystified. Their lives had taken dramatically different turns. Heather claimed to be content at home with kids; her kitchen was full of light pouring through stained glass, bright children's paintings, and she did her best to radiate calm. She home-schooled her two youngest children. She did it with patience and forbearance. She never yelled.

"You guys have enough money and enough support that you could stay home," Heather had said, while Patricia struggled with the cork on the second bottle of Chardonnay. "I mean, do you really want to live like this? You're exhausted all the time. You haven't returned my phone calls in weeks, and I haven't been able to get you out for a walk since Christmas." Heather and Patricia used to have a ritual of meeting Saturday mornings to walk through the park along the whole length of the riverbank. They had done this for several years, at first with baby strollers, and then jogging or power walking. They had joked about rollerblading, staring enviously at the teens who whizzed by them. If their husbands were amenable to having the children longer on Saturdays, Heather and Patricia would sometimes go for breakfast at the Caffe Italia. But that was before Zack. Not to mention the fact that Patricia had felt like a zombie the last few months, barely making it through the weekends, on Mondays nearly grateful to be back at work, where she at least had the illusion of order and control. Heather often reminded Patricia that she wasn't taking any time for herself anymore. By which she meant for Heather, Patricia thought. Then she immediately regretted her meanness. But staying home isn't exactly making Heather the happiest woman on earth, from the look of things. Her drinking had been steadily increasing in the past few years.

"But I'm making nearly twice as much now, and Zack's meds and all the physios and specialists are costing us a mint. Not to mention Hilary." Patricia was grateful for their live-in Australian nanny: Hilary was devoted to Max, sensing his jealousy that Zack got everyone's attention. The aroma of her homemade soup when Patricia returned from work was not just a physical welcome but a respite from maternal guilt.

"Money ain't everything," countered Heather.

"Actually, money can buy a lot," she snapped. Then she sucked in her breath, and raised her glass to Heather. "Except two things I have yet to figure out." She sipped, noting Heather's raised eyebrow, making her perfect skin and cherubic face look askew. "You can't pay someone to exercise for you. And there's something called 'parent participation' that makes me shudder when I see it on some notice Max brings home. All those good parents who come to every PAC meeting and sit through Suzuki violin

lessons and spot their kids on the trampoline make me
sick." Patricia turned her head quickly, instantly remembering that Heather was doing Suzuki with her youngest,
James. Shit, why couldn't she just bite her tongue? Too
many times lately she had found herself drinking a lot of
wine before supper. It was a habit she'd have to curb. She
spun around to face Heather, who was leaning against
the kitchen island. Heather's hand was shaking as she
reached for the stem of her glass. Patricia had teased
Heather several times about getting an early case of
Parkinson's. But really the shaking was getting worse.
Heather had smashed her wine glass putting it in the
sink before she left. Patricia wasn't sure, but she could
have sworn it was on purpose. Both of them apologized.

·～

PATRICIA'S CELLPHONE RINGS AGAIN; IT'S TUCKED
into the waistband of her sweatpants and she pulls it out
as she moves into the living room to escape Zachary's
cries, picking up Max's abandoned dirty socks off the
floor at the same time. It would have to be like this on
Hilary's day off. Where is Ron anyway? He should have
been back from the conference by now. It's Ron's parents
and they're coming Thursday night. Could she check out
the new ferry schedule and get back to them? Patricia
jots a note down on the back of a flyer advertising 2 for 1
pizza, then races toward the kitchen cupboard, reaching
for Zack's phenobarb. Then she remembers that she

already gave him a larger dose just after seven. So why hasn't it worked? Why hasn't he stopped wailing?

For Christmas, her mother had given her two gift certificates for massage therapy. For the last few days, Patricia has been close to picking up the phone to make an appointment. She can feel that all the muscles in her back and neck are tense, and she's ached for weeks. Her shoulder blades are tighter than unfurled wings; they feel skewered like a turkey's. But she fears what would happen if her body relaxed. She might embarrass herself by weeping or being unable to get up off the massage table. It would be too much. Some days she remembers how her life used to be, back when she was a university student. She could just grab her keys and wallet and walk out the door. Now, even a minor weekend excursion involves packing diapers, bottles, medications, change pad, and bundling the kids up before she even opens the door. In the winter, it's worse: Max has to pee as soon as she has him zipped into his snowsuit and into his boots.

Patricia has lost the desire to be impulsive anyway, or no longer recalls her former spontaneity. She remembers reading in a magazine about the serenity that settles upon mothers; she envies the women swathed in downy white towels in the soft, blurry photographs, holding precious infants; they look clean, calm and good. She has never felt like that. The magazines with glossy photos and titles like *New Mother* pile up neatly on the coffee table, but she never has time to read them. Once she also believed in five-year plans, in neatly defined careers and in setting goals, in keeping up subscriptions so that she could improve her mind.

What mind? If she'd half a mind, she'd have remembered that Ron's colleague was coming for supper on Friday night, and she would have had the guest room ready. Instead of standing like an idiot in sweatpants and paint-spattered sneakers, garden shears in one hand, when he had arrived at the gravelled path at the side of the house.

"Yes, may I help you?" she had said, fearing he was a Jehovah's Witness or a vacuum cleaner salesman.

"I'm Victor," he said, holding out his hand.

"Yes?" she replied, wiping her hands on her backside, grateful for the garden dirt that prevented her having to shake hands. She had placed her hands on her hips, waiting for his opening sales pitch.

"I wasn't sure if you'd be home or not, but Ron said you weren't going into the office today."

She had braced her sunglasses on top of her head and stared at the man.

"I'm sorry. Do I know you?"

"Not yet. I'm Victor Longley."

There was a little bell going off in her head. She stood stiffly and glared at his outline, the sun casting his body as a tall silhouette haloed by dappled leaves from the maple tree.

"I'm, uh, Ron's colleague. We spoke earlier on the phone. You said it was all right if I stayed over while the conference was on?" It came out as a question rather than a statement. Patricia blinked. It was there in her memory, if only dimly. What had she written it down on this time? A Post-it she would find balled-up on the bottom of the washing machine tub? The back of an envelope for another bill she'd forgotten to pay?

Somehow she had pulled together a last-minute, almost-gourmet meal, for which the men had acted overly grateful. They scurried out shortly after, citing the need to discuss some academic business. The guys had come home around 1:30, quite pissed and trailing the odour of beer and rum in with them. Ron had worked so hard to put the university conference together, and everyone in the history department had been astonished at his bringing over international scholars to give papers. His own paper had been written at the last minute — an all-nighter. Patricia had been grateful that Ron had had the chance to blow off some steam. She could use an excuse to get out some night herself. Today his face had been haggard and unshaven over the bacon and eggs, and Victor had graciously taken Max outside to play road hockey after breakfast. Apparently the conference on Friday night and Saturday had been a success, despite the morose expression of her hungover husband.

What if Heather were right? What if our kids are getting too damaged by both parents being away at work twelve hours a day? What if Zack would miraculously improve if she stayed home and touched him all day long? They'd been clear at the hospital that he would never fully recover. But they said such things about terminal cancer patients, and then scores of relatives wearing rosaries and surrounding the patient's bedside proved them wrong.

What if, as Heather had once suggested, Patricia were a workaholic because she had buried herself in books since the age of ten when she couldn't deal with her parents' divorce? Or she was hiding from her brother's suicide? God, this is just the sort of thinking that is completely useless right now, she chides herself. And she could accuse Heather of alcoholism — her hands always shaking as she reached for her drink — which was no different than workaholism, maybe worse for your health. For the next half hour, as she gathers laundry from laundry baskets around the house, she tries to dispel these thoughts from her head. Ron could wash these clothes, but she knows that he'll arrive home exhausted too and he doesn't need one more lecture about how he isn't doing his half of the work. As it is, laundry is the only chore they share, now that they've hired Hilary.

She keeps thinking about her family. Everyone has a dysfunctional family these days, and we're all bringing them out of the closets. People had stress during the Middle Ages, too, with plagues and high infant mortality rates. In comparison, contending with Zack should be a breeze. Quit complaining, she tells herself sternly, recognizing the tone of her mother's voice once more. After all, she reasons, we're all broken. Maybe the ones who are not quite as damaged have to take care of the ones who are most damaged, and that is all we can do. Zack had taught her that much. To look for any sense or blame in the grand scheme of things was simply beyond her.

Patricia clears the table, turns on the lamp, and takes the file folder from her briefcase. Woof, woof, Mr. Vern boss man, here I am, Sunday night, at your beck and call. Throw me a bone. Your faithful eager beaver, willing to give up my life for the greater cause of the Ministry and your reappointment. Why is it that in all my life I've either had time or money but never both simultaneously? Find that coffee. Wake up, girl. Time to get down to work.

Patricia wanders over to the microwave, where her coffee still awaits her in a stone-cold mug. She punches in her banking password by mistake, hits "Clear," then presses the timer for one minute. She glances at the time, sees that it is 9:31 and figures that she can get the report done and still be in bed by midnight. The microwave light comes on while the cup spins around. Patricia watches through the window as the cup rotates on the glass platter and wonders how she should shape the conclusion of the report. Greedily she sips her coffee, which disappears much too quickly. She needs a report that is vague enough that he can step in and tell the committee his own interpretation of events, while still being concise and hardhitting. Should she draw her own conclusions from the statistics the study had produced or would he find that presumptuous? She would need to brief him before the meeting and then let him decide. Should she get wasted by having more coffee?

Maybe she would carry on with Vern if he were appointed for another term. With a bit more funding in place, the eight-point campaign they had laboured over might really take off. They might be able to implement some real changes in the provincial health care system. She could envision herself, in her fantasy, helping Vern write the speech to announce the changes and then reading it to the media. Already she had learned to be more relaxed in front of the cameras. Oh, stop getting distracted, Patricia, and get down to work! What was that quotation? "We are such stuff as dreams are made of, and our little life is something something with a sleep." Patricia can't remember exactly how it goes. She remembers it from *The Tempest* at university, where she'd played Miranda in first year. What fun they had had, the whole cast, after rehearsals, going out for drinks and talking until dawn. Of course then she'd been able to sleep until noon the next day, even if she missed a class. It was always possible to get the notes from someone else. Right now she would like to get notes from someone, some instructions, some manual on how to prepare for her life.

Patricia sees Hilary's sweater hanging on the back of the dining room chair. She will be at her sister's house, relaxing and enjoying her day off. Sitting down at the dining room table, Patricia glances around. When did the dining room become a flat filing cabinet? Oh well, they only had formal dinners at Thanksgiving and Christmas. Zachary is fidgeting in his crib upstairs. Thrashing, to be precise. Then it dies down. Patricia turns her attention back to the report. She should proofread it first for typos. When is Ron going to get home anyway? Why have they been gone so long? The thumping noises coming through the ceiling get louder, and Patricia sighs, takes off her glasses and places them beside her coffee cup. Why the panicked hope that Zack's naps would last longer? Why the sense that she had been turned into some kind of mechanical nursemaid who went up and down stairs to switch on the light in his room at irregular intervals?

Patricia shuffles up the stairs in her stocking feet, listens at Max's door as she passes down the hallway toward Zack's crib. They had rearranged their bedrooms after bringing him home from the pediatrics ward. Patricia's mother had come to decorate the nursery and sew curtains two months before Zack's birth. But now the crib had been moved into the walk-in closet in the master bedroom; it saved steps in the middle of the night. She has the path between the bed and the crib in her visceral memory bank. At night, when she moved in her sleep from the warmth of her sheets toward the cold limbs of her son — Zack always threw the blankets off — she felt like a zombied Sisyphus. Was she being punished? Had she and Ron done something wrong? Was it that extra glass of wine she'd had at Ron's birthday party when she was pregnant? A mistake in her previous life? Although Patricia has decided that such questions are useless, they circulate in her brain when fatigue nestles in her body. Wearily she picks her squirming son up and talks to him slowly.

"What is it, Zack? Are you trying to tell me something? Are you going to have another fit soon? Mmm? You keep changing the way you want to tell me that something's wrong. Trying to keep Mommy on her toes, huh?"

Zack wiggles his arms and strains against her. There is mucus clogging his nose, which Patricia wipes with a tissue. The phenobarb has done nothing to alleviate his crying. She paces across the room, holding his frame lightly. He weighs so little, but Patricia would swear that he doubles his body weight when he goes rigid with spasms. She tries to show him the view out the bedroom window and his head rolls back into the crook of her arm.

"Look at all the beautiful new green buds. Did you know that it's springtime right now? Maybe in the morning Hilary will take you for a walk to the market and you can get some more apples for that yummy applesauce you like so much. Would you like that? We'll put on the new sun hat that Gramma gave you."

Zack is not mollified. He arches his neck and wails loudly. Okay then, thinks Patricia, we'll keep you warm and calm you down the way the pediatric nurse recommended. She marches down the stairs, gripping his legs against her chest. Turning the corner, Patricia heads down to the laundry room in the basement. She switches on the overhead fluorescent light, and they are bathed in blue. He is momentarily startled into silence. Zack blinks his long lashes rapidly and then cries even louder. Patricia puts him in the car seat on top of the washing machine and snaps the buckles into place under his crotch and across his chest. She reaches with one hand for her jacket, hanging on the peg. She slips on her sandals, swings her purse off the hook, and opens the carport door, the car seat with Zack in it balanced on her hip. After she has her son settled in the back of the car, she takes a moment to arrange a blanket over him. This time he cannot fling it off; she has learned how to tuck it under the car seat straps so that he cannot reach the edges.

Patricia croons low and evenly after she turns on the engine, which offers a background hum. She wishes she were stalwart. Maybe just for a moment, if she sucks her breath in slowly and exhales all the bad thoughts, peace will descend upon her. Zack will pick up all her good vibrations and fall asleep. If she could only make a habit of this, they could develop a symbiotic rhythm and console each other. If she flooded his room with Bach and the right aromatherapy oils filtered through the air constantly, Zack would feel bliss and would not cry.

Slowly Patricia backs the station wagon out of the driveway, remembering too late that she has not yet put the trash cans out on the side of the driveway for the morning pickup. She must remember to do so on the way back into the house. She shifts into drive and the engine purrs as the car moves slowly down the avenue. She brakes briefly for stop signs, anxious to find a long stretch of road where she will not have to stop and jar Zack in the car seat. It is 10:20 by the dashboard clock, little green monster numbers, Max calls them. Please God, let this work. She has even resorted to plea bargaining. I will do anything You ask. Why didn't I grab my coffee on the way out? And I'm hungry again. A slice of toast for me when I get him back to bed. And some of those peach preserves I picked up at the market last week, the jar decorated with maroon ribbon and a gingham hat.

Patricia thinks enviously of Heather's pantry, where there are shelves of homemade pickles and preserves in colourful columns, all made by Heather and the kids, labelled with stickers they've designed on the computer. Once she had made the mistake of bringing a large jar of pickled carrots, pearl onions, baby corns and green peppers to Heather's house as an offering.

"Pat, do you mean you finally took a day off to do these up?" Heather had asked.

"Um, no, I stopped at Costco yesterday," Patricia had mumbled.

"Oh. There's no tag or label, so I couldn't tell."

When she was a child, Patricia had enjoyed her visits with her grandmother, who always presented Patricia with a jar of something delicious: honey was her favourite, but it might also be apricots or peaches from her Gramma's backyard. Patricia would beg her mother for vanilla ice cream or fresh whipped cream and spoon the fruit on top of the white clouds, then slowly blend in the fruit in small, delicate circles until she achieved a new colour. It was like mixing paint at school, more pleasurable than eating. Something Zack will never experience. Or maybe his palate does discriminate. Who knows?

He whimpers in the back seat.

"Keep it down to a dull roar until we hit the highway," says Patricia. In the rearview, she can see that his nose and mouth are covered in snot again, but there is a small grin on his face. Zachary loves car rides.

"Take me for a ride in your car car, take me for a ride in your car-car. Take me for a ride, take me for a ride. Take me for a ride in your car-car," Patricia sings. Songs from Max's cassette tapes circulate in her brain continually. Often at work she will find herself humming, "If you're happy and you know it, clap your hands" or "Poor little bug on the wall, nobody loves him at all." When was the last time she and Ron had lain on the couch together and listened to their music? Heather had given her a new Van Morrison CD last Christmas that she hasn't even had time to listen to yet, but still her mind is full of nursery rhymes and bedtime songs. "Oh, Sam-I-am, it's you again," was her line when Ron used to sneak up on her from behind. "Bring me your green eggs and ham." Phonetic foreplay. God, how many months since they'd played that game? And even were Ron to have the energy to do so now, she suspected she would find it more annoying than endearing.

Sometimes, Ron used to crawl into bed beside her, where she was usually reading reports, her briefcase propped up on her knees. Playfully he would slide the briefcase off the futon and onto the floor and run his hands inside her thighs, chanting, "Could you, would you, on a train? Not on a train! Not in a tree! Not in a car! Sam! Let me be! I would not, could not, in a box. I could not, would not, with a fox."

Zachary is humming a snot-filled song, sending drops of moisture onto his jacket. Five more minutes and he'll be out, prays Patricia. Heather is right, I need a break. Ron booked a flight to Puerto Vallarta in November, but that seems so far away. They will go to Club Med this time — not exactly their style, but the kids' programs for Max were attractive. And it's sunny outside now that spring's here. She should be outside enjoying the weather. Not that she could have a holiday in the summer when normal people do. And so she turns her mind to Mexico. All she wants is sun, a book, hot sand, cold ocean and a drink before dusk. To sleep, to swim, to fuck, to eat. Keep it simple. And she might actually finish reading the novel she'd started over a month ago.

She is coasting along the highway, driving too fast. She looks again in the rearview and sees that Zack has finally dropped off to sleep. Patricia turns right at the next exit and heads back toward the city centre. Heather had snorted when Patricia had told her about the Club Med.

"But don't you want to see the real Mexico?"

"No, I don't want to see anything. Except my painted toes sticking out of the sand."

"Wow, you've changed so much since you and Ron went backpacking in Nepal. But I guess I can see it, when you're so burned out from your job. But what about Zack?"

"We'll leave him with Hilary for the ten days."

"Nice you can do that, at least."

"Yeah, well, it's not like we have a lot of choice, with all his doctor appointments and checkups," Patricia responded rather defensively.

"Well, I envy you. Mexico in November, when there's nothing but slushy streets here. It'll give you something to look forward to."

Patricia knows that Heather envies her nothing, is merely being polite. If she wanted to, Heather could leave her kids with her mother and go to Montreal, where she and Bob had honeymooned, anytime she liked, for Chrissakes. But Heather maintains that she didn't need holidays, that being with her kids is gratifying and not nearly as stressful as when she had played in the orchestra for next to no pay. Heather is the sort of woman who actually takes pleasure from sewing all her children's Halloween costumes every year, staying up at the sewing machine late into the night. She's also big on reducing stress, constantly offering Patricia advice on everything from B complex to strategies for combatting PMS. Dairy products are, according to Heather, as evil as pesticides, and she feeds her children only organic fruit. Some days Patricia comes home to find a box of spotted apples on the doorstep and recognizes Heather's calling card. Max would take one bite of an apple and pitch it into the trash, maintaining that he couldn't eat wormy apples. Patricia chides him for being wasteful, but is too tired to pursue the matter. That might be the whole problem, of course. Patricia glanced around the interior of the car, which was, as usual, littered with take-out food bags, plastic straws and cup lids. Maybe if she'd read all the labels on all the foods she'd eaten when she was pregnant, things might have turned out differently. Dioxins in the plastic wrap that she put on everything in the microwave caused genetic mutations in fish. Her genes constantly being mutated and bombarded. And it wasn't even something she could see. Like the radioactive waves from her computer hitting her underwire bra and giving her breast cancer next. Zap. Just like that.

Patricia turns into the carport slowly, trying not to let any movement wake Zachary. Ron's car is still not in the drive. Gently she lifts out the car seat, listening to the seat belt slither and click back into place. My child smells like a medicine cabinet, she thinks, as she presses him against her chest and then carries the car seat by the handle toward the basement door. As the handle locks into place, Zachary is startled awake. Shit, thinks Patricia guiltily.

By the time she has the door unlocked, Zack is screaming blue murder. She sets the car seat on top of the dryer and turns it on. After it kicks in, warmth emanates through the metal and the vibrations rattle the seat. Zachary is instantly calm. "One day I'm accidentally going to put you in the dryer instead of on it," Patricia muses. She looks around the basement, sees the old dusty card table folded up against the wall. Now she just needs a chair.

"Stay right there, sweetie. Mommy will be right back." Yeah. Like he's really going to run off somewhere. She takes the stairs two at a time. In the kitchen, Patricia grabs her pen and flings it into her briefcase, which she snaps shut and pulls toward her with one hand. With the other hand, she drags a kitchen chair and hauls it toward the stairs, thumping it behind her as she descends. Zachary's eye seems to follow her.

"See, told you I'd only be a second. God, I am so dumb! What if you'd had another seizure and fallen off the dryer? Oh, thank God you're still here!" Patricia is seized with remorse and covers Zachary's face with kisses. He is warm and damp.

"Good boy! Mommy is going to do her work right beside you so you can get some sleep. See? I'm just going to set this table up so I can put my work on it. There we go. You do love that dryer, don't you? Ye-es."

Zachary is cooing and spitting happily. The chair seat only gives Patricia six inches clearance for her knees. Oh, well, she thinks. She turns her attention back to the report, and is soon absorbed in rewriting the conclusion. She crumples rough notes into balls of paper and hurls them into the wastepaper basket beside the washing machine, sending balls of lint flying into the air. Most of her aims are bad, and a small fort of paper builds up on the concrete floor at the foot of the washing machine.

Finally, Patricia lifts her head. She slips the pages into her briefcase and clicks it shut. It is 2:31 AM by the digital clock beside the washing machine. She has just poured a second cup of liquid Tide instead of fabric softener into the washer, but does not realize her mistake until all the dirty clothes are loaded and the cycle has begun. Huge bubbles leak out beyond the lid of the washing machine and drool down the sides, spilling onto the floor. Patricia flips open the lid and shouts, crying, into the mountain of suds. But the clothes continue to swirl around and around the agitator, rocked from side to side. Now she is sobbing, the noisy rhythms of the machine drowning out her voice. When she lifts her head at last, she sees that Zachary has finally fallen asleep soundly on top of the dryer, and gently she shifts the weight of his warm body from the car seat onto her shoulder. His snoring is a soft buzzing sound in her ear, and his mouth twitches into a brief smile. The washing machine has shifted into the spin cycle, and the clothes continue to whirl around and around. Patricia clings to the small boy whose body is wrapped against hers, and slowly waltzes across the concrete floor, spinning around and around and around.

To Rise Above

IT WAS NOT THAT THEY WEREN'T WELL-INTENTIONED. But Linda wished that all the visitors who kept arriving at her bed during visiting hours would notice her fatigue and vanish as quickly as they had appeared. Linda closed one eye, then the other, when someone stood beside her food tray, making the bodies shift from one corner of the bed to the other. This was a game she had often played as a child when adults began to bore her. Like her Uncle Thomas, who would always say the same thing when greeting her: "That's my little Linda. Would've recognized you anywhere." But not even Uncle Thomas could have recognized her now. She surveyed her body in the moments between the intrusion of visitors, lifting the cool white sheets to gaze at blue bruises blooming across her flesh like flowers entwining the trellis of her ribs, six of which were cracked and carefully taped together. Both her eyes were blackened and stared back at her in the mirror from sunken holes in her face. Perhaps what embarrassed her most were the brilliant red slashes and welts along her throat and neck, impossible to hide from view. Linda woke up every morning and examined her bruises, pleased to note the fading colours. But the red marks along her throat, she realized, would require months of wearing scarves, what her mother called "tasteful accessorizing" of her wardrobe.

Linda felt numb. She often felt numb. She had no family, no relations, in this cold wintry city. The job drew her here, but she had not warmed up to the city. Even after two years, she couldn't bring herself to purchase property, was not sure whether or not she wanted to make a long-term commitment. To anyone or anything. Even getting her cat Simpson had been a tough decision. Now the city felt even more alien. *I am getting out of here,* she thought. What just happened is a sign and I should pay attention to it.

Kim had been the first to arrive today; she had made daily trips to offer Linda sympathy and advice, to check the healing of her bruises. Linda recognized her voice down the hall, arguing with a nurse who was insisting that no visitors would be admitted until he had finished administering all the meds. Kim was bellowing some- thing about speaking to his superiors, and bus schedules, her voice rising and falling like a wave before it crashed at the door to Linda's room, which she kicked open, her arms full of books and papers. Linda winced, glancing at the other three beds in the room to see if the other patients had been disturbed, but the two older women were glued to a game show on the blaring television, and the third bed appeared to be rumpled but empty. She stretched her arms and legs in opposing directions between the sheets, trying to flex her muscles, wincing at the pain.

Kim worked as a counsellor at the Rape Crisis Centre; she and Linda had become close friends after Linda had volunteered at a community benefit for the centre. But Linda believed their friendship continued more from obligation than affection. Kim seemed intent on making Linda aware that the world was, as she put it, more "politicized" than Linda realized. "There are forces out there at work that we need to come to grips with," she was fond of telling Linda, "and you can't live the rest of your life with your head in the sand." Linda's role seemed to be to follow Kim's lead, especially at the meetings she attended with her, and to be flattered when Kim introduced her as "the only woman bank manager in town." Linda was never certain if, in calling her that, Kim was in part apologizing for Linda's appearance, as if the designer suits and heels that she favoured were only a corporate disguise. In fact, Linda loved dressing up, but she always went along with Kim's assumption that she was merely embodying essential camouflage, that this was one of the ugly necessities of women's survival in the corporate world. When she joined Kim and some of her other women friends for a drink after these meetings, she always felt a bit reckless, daring, as if she borrowed by osmosis their more radical dress for the occasion.

Kim strode purposefully toward her now, setting down the books and papers at the edge of the bed before drawing a chair alongside her. "Poor Linda," she said solemnly. She had been to visit several days ago and to offer her condolences, but now she had that "take charge" look that Linda recognized. She had always admired Kim's decisiveness, her certitude that any problem could be solved, that there was a right and a wrong and that right would always win, with persistence. Kim plumped Linda's pillows behind her, then lowered Linda's shoulders firmly back onto the pillows.

"I never thought I'd have to see you in my professional capacity. Now I wish I'd been more insistent about signing you up for one of our self-defence courses. I blame myself, you know. It took me so long to unlearn all those years of training in passivity. I should have recognized that you just needed more of a push."

Linda shifted her legs awkwardly. The books were pulling the bedspread down, constricting her movement. She looked at Kim's flushed face, smelled the cold she had brought in the room with her, and felt envious of the normal frenzy of winter life that was flourishing outside the hospital when everything in the ward seemed oddly languid, suspended. She pictured a frozen landscape inside a crystal globe, like the one she had played with as a child. Out there must be couples sleepy beneath the cloak of winter's inactivity, suddenly throwing aside their eiderdowns, suddenly alive, shaken up, a blizzard in a glass. While she could only lie here, immobile under fluorescent tubes.

Very little detail remained in Linda's mind. It was as if the attack had happened to someone else, in another lifetime. Linda remembered removing the paper grocery bags from the trunk of her Toyota, slamming the lid down and hearing the hollow, squeaking echo as the noise reverberated in the concrete underground parking lot below her apartment block. She recalled shifting the heavier bag, the one containing the milk jug, from one hip to the other, and simultaneously feeling something tighten across her chest. At first Linda believed that she had caught her purse strap around one of the grocery bags. It wasn't until she smelled his sour breath on her neck and saw the glint of the knife in the corner of her eye that she had noticed his arm pressing against her diaphragm. Then she felt the panic rising from her belly, the taste of her own bile, and a dull pounding at the back of her throat.

He told her what he was going to do to her before he did it. Told her she deserved it. That if she screamed she would just make it harder for herself. Linda had not screamed. Even with his full weight on top of her as he pushed her toward the concrete floor, even as she felt the buttons on her blouse pop against the strain of her arms pinned beneath her while he slashed the rest of her clothing off with the knife, she said nothing. She felt her mind drifting up to the roof of the concrete parking lot. She noticed the cold of the concrete floor against her burning cheek, forced herself to feel nothing else but cold. When the pain was most intense, when it seemed as though he would never finish with her, she willed herself to focus on the details of objects around her that assumed a luminous intensity. Watching oranges roll under the axles of adjacent cars or observing the upturned yogurt container ooze its white sludge into an iridescent oil puddle on the concrete, Linda realized that she would have no time to order birthday flowers for her mother that afternoon. She could think of nothing else but her daily planner and what she had pencilled in for the next few days. Mentally she began rearranging her dental appointment and her aerobics classes, trying to determine which of her late meetings next week she could safely miss. Phrases like "unforeseen circumstances" clouded her thoughts. She would call her boss tomorrow, she thought, as she heard her own teeth crunch in her ear and tasted blood. She sighted a single glossy McIntosh rolling only slightly beyond her grasp and focused on its label, as if discerning the place of origin of the apple were of the utmost importance. Then she passed out.

Kim must have sensed Linda drifting away. Her hand was now stroking Linda's hair in a gentle way that reminded Linda of one of her favourite childhood games: playing "Mermaid Hairdresser" with her sister. But then she involuntarily pulled her head back, her neck growing stiff, repulsed by Kim's touch. "I brought you some of these to read," Kim said, kindly, and then her voice took on its light, joking tone.

"Hey, at least you don't live in Babylon. There, if you were a virgin and engaged and were raped, of course it wouldn't be your fault, so your attacker would be killed. But if you were a married woman and raped, look out — both you and your attacker were thrown into the river to drown! If you weren't engaged or married, you were just asking for it, so you would deserve death. Too much, eh? Lucky for you that you were born in this decade, given that you haven't even gotten engaged and have wasted your miserable life making oodles of money in a fancy career."

Linda caught the sarcasm masking Kim's compliment, or at least she thought it was a compliment; she felt the breeziness of Kim's wit and was grateful. Most people found Kim obnoxious and hard to take. Linda was by turns exasperated by and fond of Kim's foibles. But she was also aware of feeling too calm, as if Kim's words were dulled by some tape recorder being played at slow speed. It could be the tranquilizers, she thought. Why can't I even cry?

"Here," continued Kim. "I saved this one from our newsletter from last month. Check this out: 'How to Avoid Rape: Don't go out without clothes. That encourages men. Don't go out with clothes — any clothes encourage some men. Avoid childhood — some rapists are turned on by the very young. Avoid old age — some rapists prefer older women. Don't have a father, grandfather, uncle or brother — these are the relatives who most often rape women. Don't marry. To be quite safe, don't exist!" Kim snickered. She was trying to be lighthearted and Linda appreciated her effort. Only it hurt her face to laugh. Kim told her about the potluck coming up, tempting her with the promise of bringing potato salad, a recipe she teasingly wouldn't give her even though Linda was crazy about it. She talked heartily about the meals they would cook together when Linda got out. It would be good to taste real food again after hospital swill. A night at the best Greek restaurant, Kim promised before she left. Tzatziki and hummus. Lots of retsina.

Kim had not asked her for details on her first visit, nor did she press her now. Mercifully. Linda could have offered no description of her attacker. In any case, with some of her teeth missing, she could barely speak. Now she would need to make several visits to the dentist. And she hadn't even been able to cancel her last appointment in time. Would she be billed for it? Why was she thinking about that now? Why couldn't she just say goodbye cordially to Kim, whose farewell wave looked more like a salute?

Martha did not ask her for particulars either. She arrived just before the end of visiting hours, walked slowly toward Linda's bed until Linda could smell the cold outdoors on Martha's coat as she unbuttoned it and pulled a chair over to the bed. She looked puzzled and awkward, as if unsure what to say to Linda.

"Are you feeling any better yet?" Martha asked in her usual quiet, shy manner. She was too nervous to say much, perhaps. Which suited Linda just fine. She was tired of having to explain the mixture of feelings she was having. Swear words coming in a torrent into her mind, molten and angry. The limp, rag-doll feeling when all she wanted was for someone big and strong to lift her and hold her. She was useless, like a child waiting to be told what to do next. Full of aches that she wanted someone to kiss to make the pain go away. Ashamed to be so weak, telling everyone she was fine even though it was obvious to anyone that she was pretending. She felt embarrassed to be seen in the shabby hospital gown, with no makeup on, in front of gorgeous Martha.

"You look absolutely marvellous. Where did you get that dress?" said Linda. Only it came out as "dreth," her lips swollen. Not only did she look like shit, but she couldn't even speak properly now. Just great.

"Mmm, isn't it terrific? I got it at the Sally Ann for two dollars." Martha had no idea how beautiful she was. She possessed a gentle charm that seemed to render her invulnerable to those deviously inventive insecurities that plagued Linda. So it electrified the air when Martha leaned over her and lowered her voice to speak..

"You know, I don't talk about it much anymore, but it happened to me too, when I was fifteen." Her smile pulled tautly at the sides of her face, her cheeks crimson. Linda was unable to respond, not even a pathetic murmur.

And then Martha gave Linda a gift. As if to recover her composure quickly when Linda had not responded to her confession, she drew out the badly rumpled plastic shopping bag from under her chair. Of course it was another of Martha's "treasures," as she called them, her "scores" from one of the local thrift stores. And from a paper bag she pulled a small cardboard box of ripe plums, out of season, juicy and inviting. She leaned over and held one out to Linda.

"I found the plums in Chinatown and I couldn't walk by them without my mouth watering. And as for this other bag, well, I remembered you had the same size as me from that day we went skating," Martha said, pulling a pair of leather boots out of the bag. Linda absent-mindedly thanked her. Martha left hurriedly, saying that visiting hours were over and she had to run and catch her bus. All these damn buses coming and going, Linda thought, while I'm lying here, going nowhere fast.

Martha, a teller at Linda's bank, was generous to a fault. They had only known each other for a couple of years, had lunch twice. Martha had insisted on paying both times, even though Linda obviously made more money than her. At the office skating party, they had both sat in the bleachers blowing on their hot cocoas to cool them down, talking about their childhood skating lessons. Their talk was easy, comfortable. But it was awkward developing relationships with people she had to be in charge of, Linda told herself, more professional not to mix business with friendship. She had been mistrustful of Martha at first, overwhelmed by her sensual but casual beauty, uncertain why she had been chosen to be this stunning creature's friend. But Martha wanted nothing from her. And now these gifts from someone she had ignored. She regretted not having returned Martha's generosity. Linda vowed to make more time for her as soon as she got out of this hospital bed and back into action. She remembered how fast she moved at work, how often she paced in her office when she had to make a decision. The bank employees teased her by calling her Road Runner.

Now she was filled with a swift anger that she was unable to move her ribs and walk. More damned self-pity was useless. Sometimes the flashbacks knitted themselves together, flowed over in an uninvited sequence that she felt helpless to stop. The knife glinting in the light. The McIntosh apple rolling toward her. White yogurt being muddied by dark oil. Stains that could never be removed. It must have been something wrong she did, she mused as she drifted off toward sleep again. She wouldn't be feeling so badly now if only she had got something right, but she wasn't sure what it was. Maybe it would come back to her ...

A WEEK LATER, IT WAS TIME FOR LINDA TO GO home. Learning that she had no family there, the orderly

offered to call one of Linda's friends to come and pick
her up, but Linda obstinately refused, wanting instead
to get on a bus. To get home by herself seemed important, to prove to herself that she was okay. She doubted
she would ever be able to get into her own car again. No,
she did not want a cab, she told the orderly. She couldn't
bear having to make small talk with the driver. She dressed
slowly, pulling out the clothing Kim had picked up from
Linda's apartment from the large plastic drawstring bag
that the nurse had carried to her bedside table along with
a release form for her signature. And then she sighted the
boots again. She pulled the right one on over her stockinged
calf and stretched it to its full length; the brown leather
was smooth, well-worn, soft, and the square chunky heel
felt solid below her foot, even though she tottered on the
other leg. It gave her a sensation of being enclosed, almost
protected, from the knee down, and she realized it felt
foreign to be wearing something on her feet after sliding
along the waxed floors in paper hospital slippers for so
many days. With the second boot on, she felt balanced
again, sturdy. She even tried stomping them, and giggled
softly. And had a recollection of an old childhood desire,
a longing that held her gaze transfixed to the same page in
the Eaton's catalogue every fall, fascinated by the gleaming,
tall, zip-up leather boots (would she choose brown or
black?) that cost more than she could ever save up from
her babysitting money, more than her mother would ever

spend on a Christmas present. Invariably each fall, she received a pair of lined vinyl boots, because her mother always insisted they were the most "practical," that leather would be destroyed by salt and snow. She remembered the heeled cowboy boots she had bought with her first paycheque as a waitress. But these boots from Martha were reminiscent of the ones from the catalogue all those years ago: calf-hugging, sleek, impossibly tall.

As soon as she found a seat on the bus, Linda began shivering irrepressibly. The shivers turned into occasional twitches as she adjusted to the heat blasting from the wall of the bus. By the time she stepped down from the bus, she found herself laughing quietly. Holding the large plastic sack labelled GARMENT BAG in one hand, she stood at the edge of the subdivision just as the day began to fade. She heard the engine of the bus roar in the distance as it pulled away, and was frightened by the hollowness of her giggling in the sudden stillness. There were two blocks to walk before she could reach her apartment building, but between the single-family dwellings and her high-rise was a developer's no man's land, a zone of indeterminate space where a hayfield and a small stand of trees gave some suggestion of the land's agricultural origins. Almost pastoral. All that's missing are a few cows, she thought.

The snow was folded like a soft baby's blanket across the field, occasional thatches of dry hay poking through at the seams. In this late afternoon light, the snow was the colour of skim milk, a gentle curve of pale blue-white that emphasized the robin's-egg blue of the sky. The air was growing perceptibly colder against her skin. The boughs of the trees hung humbly under the weight of velvet snow, waiting to spring back into shape when delivered of their burden, the soft thud of snow tumbling to the ground. From below Linda's rib cage came a gradual release, a deep exhalation, unbidden. She was no longer shivering, even though she was passing a darker wooded area now, and the last of the sun's rays were momentarily blocked. She focused ahead on the tall apartment building that used to feel like her home. She did not know what she expected to feel when she arrived there, that high-rise in the sky. But she pushed through the snow that had formed a hard crust on the surface, and each of her footsteps made a sharp crunch. The snap, snap of the snow that gave way under her feet absorbed her mind and she concentrated only on taking one step after another, not looking up for a long time. When she finally lifted her head, the scene was altered.

From behind the trees, the angels emerged. The air was suddenly curdled with humidity. There were hundreds of angels, some stately and graceful, wings outstretched; and others squat, dignified and assured. Some of them resembled her friends, Linda realized in awe. Each was surrounded by a luminescence that seemed to be drawn from the sunlight's play on the snow. The full colours of the spectrum traced the outline of each shape. The angels formed two columns, flanking her on either side. Linda felt tall and strong in her new boots, placing one foot in front of the other, leaving a firm imprint in the snow.

The Traveller's Hat

What sets a canoeing expedition apart is that it purifies
you more rapidly and inescapably than any other.
Travel a thousand miles by train and you are a brute;
pedal five hundred on a bicycle and you remain basi-
cally a bourgeois; paddle a hundred in a canoe and you
are already a child of nature.
— Pierre Elliot Trudeau, "Exhaustion and Fulfillment:
The Ascetic in a Canoe" (1944)

And though it in the centre sit,
Yet when the other far doth roam,
It leans, and hearkens after it,
And grows erect as that comes home.

Such wilt thou be to me, who must
Like th' other foot, obliquely run;
Thy firmness makes my circle just,
And makes me end, where I begun.

— *John Donne, "A Valediction:*
Forbidding Mourning"

DEAR HERMES,

Can you imagine, this stupid travel guide I am reading says, "Women should avoid travelling alone!" It's been several weeks since I have written to you, but I have not forgotten you, darling. It's just that I have been so busy! I know I promised to return to you before I turned forty so we could plan our family. Already I imagine what a perfect baby we will have, one who will look like both of us, combine our best features. Who cares what sex it is? (Androgynous would be terrific.) Last night I was listening to Handel's *Messiah* and I felt the Hallelujah chorus ripple down my thighs, send a shiver up my spine, and all I could think of was you and what you do to me. For now I can only dream about the never-ending flight of future days!

The whole town is getting ready for Christmas, putting up decorations. Some days I wonder why I'm doing this, what song in my heart made me fold up my sheets, sell off my furniture and let the wind blow me here. Why is it that I can never resolve that conflict between my earth-bound body and my vagrant, nomadic mind? (Except to move my body and still my heart.) I was always like that before: running back and forth from the arms of Dionysus, who had his weapons, or Apollo, who least knew how to use his weapons! (Long before I met you, my dear pagan Hermes.) You know that I have my own journey to make, as I have insisted all the years that we have been together. I have my reliable guidebook here in front of me. I have your image always before me. I have your footsteps. I have your voice in my head, and I am always talking to you, my love. I think of you, and all the magic medicine I get from my sweet Mercury. Seeds of love. How you gave me my voice. How I feel my heart opening just a little more each day, like the lid of that box that some advise is best kept shut, but you keep urging me to crack wide open.

The concert was terrific, in the open air, with the stars out shining in all their glory. Enough to put old cares to flight. It was a full *son et lumière* performance, and the acoustics were perfect. It was as if you were the conductor and, with each crescendo, the cells of my body rose to meet your wand. Later we all staggered around the town, and I saw portraits of you atop all the stone herms at the entrances to houses; you'd have been pleased with how big they made your dick in this town! Oh companion of dark night, my furtive Hermes, I miss you so much! I know that my sorrow is just self-indulgence, the extravagance of too much time to think. I would follow you anywhere, chase your footsteps backward in time until I was reconnected with the gods. Except that I know I must follow my own journey, even if it leads me to Hades and back.

Love, Pandora

☞ **The three most important things about travelling: pack light, always wear comfortable shoes and SMILE!**

Hello again Hermes!
My face hurts from smiling so much. And oh, what I would not give to have you massage my aching feet! How you cradle my arches between your hands when you come home from work, kiss my insteps. My arms are sore from paddling, my face is sunburned, and the blackflies are going for my scalp again. But then I dip my paddle in the water (the paddle you carved me for my birthday), watch the ripples after my J stroke, and can almost see your face in the reflection of sun, trees, moon, earth. The starry heaven above that plain! Already I am a child of nature, moving down the estuary toward the sea.

And what are you smiling about these days? Are you remembering when you were pining for Aphrodite and Zeus took pity on you, sending an eagle to snatch up one of her slippers while she was bathing in the river? She wouldn't have let you make love to her if you hadn't returned the slipper after the eagle brought it to you in Egypt. What were you doing in Egypt anyway? Maybe I don't want to know. At least you set the eagle in the sky.

I smile when I think of the day you brought me the wild irises and tiger lilies and Queen Anne's lace you picked in the ditch beside the highway on your way home from work, how you laid them in my lap like an offering, a promise that winter would soon end. It was the finest gift I have received. Any other man would have thoughtlessly bought me a dozen red roses. I have always counted upon you to keep your imagination alive, so that I can flourish too. There are trilliums along the bank of the river, crouching in the shade. When I extinguished my campfire last night, I heard them whispering to me.

How often you have teased me about my flightiness! I think that you secretly enjoy that about me, that it makes you feel centred and strong, pointing out your sturdiness to me like a wise tree extending its branch. Sweetheart, the tree may be rooted but its branches point in all directions. The truth is that I am grounded in my own fashion, but that I have always felt torn between staying put and rambling. Please understand: I am not fleeing. But my restlessness pulls me away from you, at the same time I crave your closeness. And the longer the time that has passed since I saw you, the more often I encounter you in all the men I meet. Each of them embodies one of your best attributes, makes me love you more than ever. I am always tracing your shape on the back of restaurant placemats, considering maps that might lead me back to you. But we both agreed I am not ready to settle down. Not yet.

I think of the angle of your shoulders today, the smell of your skin in the warm sun where we lie on our blanket beside the water every summer, sand clinging to our nest of discarded clothing, fruit peels, damp towels and sunscreen bottles. How I love to lean against you in the heat of the sun! And now I have only the shoulder of the road to lean on. Your accent rings in my ear, sings my name. How sweet this deprivation!

I am cutting my own trail in this backwoods. I am glad you told me to pack the machete. There are wild strawberries creeping in vines along the ground, tiny and sweet. I've got my perfect travelling shoes — a.k.a. "sensible shoes." They are just the kind I once told my mother I would never wear. I tread the earth lightly.

Love, Pandora

☞ **In India, men generally don't shake hands with women. They greet them by placing the palms of their hands together and bowing slightly.**

My dearest Hermes,

Paying for my train ticket, my hand brushed against the palm of the clerk and a shudder ran through me. It is so long since a man has touched me. Life on the road for women is simply a different trip.

Here I am, "comin' in on a wing and a prayer." I have been on this train for three days. Men get on and get off. The women wonder out loud why there is no man travelling with me: No husband? No brother? No uncle? They feel pity for me, and their men regard me as a whore. Can't they see you hovering over me? My traveller. *Mon voyageur.* You are the one who took me under his wing, my sweet Hermes. How can I tell you how much I long for you? Conductor of my soul, I hold your staff and make my wishes, while you help me make them come true. For you I would do anything, move anywhere.

Love, Pandora

 In the Pacific Islands, a woman's thighs are considered an erotic part of her body and should not be exposed in public.

Dearest love,
I am always travelling toward you. Take me home, Hermes. Tonight I am tired and I have had too much to drink. I feel fucked up and run down. I am trying to get ready for your return. No one has touched me in days, and the men stare at my unveiled head and spit on the ground when I meet their eyes. I can feel your hands all over me when I lie down to sleep at night, smell your sweat after you have lain on top of me, and I think I will die if I do not see you soon. Your incarnations are everywhere. I wish one of

them would say kindly to me, as you did, "Pandora, what would I do without your big thighs as my pillow?" I have the urge to walk naked through the streets, roll my round fleshy hips in the open air. God help me!

Love, Pandora

☞ **In India, a female's upper arms are considered sensual areas of the body and therefore must never be exposed in public.**

If you strap on wings and wrap the ties around your shoulders, this will not be a problem. Wings also provide a quick getaway from crowded bus and train platforms. In bed, remove the wings when you lie underneath your lover; soar above him when you are wearing them.

Pull the shawl around your shoulders a little tighter, and remember the day you ate tapas in the café on the street in the sunshine. Recall the sensation of olive oil dribbling down your arms where he rubbed it on you, daring you to protest in front of the other diners. Eat your meals slowly and thoughtfully, and remain covered. Laugh secretly to yourself.

Dear Hermes,

Do you remember I told you that I met a shallow man who thought I was a sparrow with a broken wing? He thought I needed rescuing, but I was wearing my feathered hat and flew away from him. I fear not, for I am of more value than many sparrows, and there is special providence in the fall of a sparrow anyway. It was not love, Hermes — you could have told me that, had I known you then. I just get a little cockstruck from time to time, led astray, distracted by that beautiful wand being waved in front of my face. It makes me lose my focus, makes me want to believe, with the naïve faith of my childhood, the lies men tell me, especially when they say they will never leave me. Thank heavens I got back on track at last, focused on my work again. Part of what you and I used to laugh about all the time — that Divine Dissatisfaction that keeps us on our own journeys.

Fondly, Pandora

☞ **To avoid extra stress, travel early in the day, especially if you don't have reservations. This gives you time to find a place you like before it gets dark. Never accept a room if the check-in clerk calls out your name or room number. Others within hearing distance may use this information to try to call you or gain access to your room.**

Dear Hermes,
You call to me in the deep bass notes of market hawkers, of megaphones that call me to bend on my knees to Allah. Oh darling, that night you crept into my room and raised the mosquito net! I was still stirring from my

sleep when your lips grazed the back of my neck. Instantly I was alert to you. How did you find the key, and how did you know I would be there, hot and pleasantly drowsy from my bath? "Open up the box and look inside," you told me, handing me your present after we made love. I wanted to ask for more. Maybe you would think that was asking too much. After all, you are my Divine Intelligence. Ficino got you all wrong, sweetheart. But how curiosity always gets the better of us!

Love, Pandora

☞ **In Saudi Arabia, a single woman doesn't drive a rental car. She must have a male driver.**

Ah, thrice-great Hermes! How I want a city man, a jazz man who will take me to all the concerts. To drive me (crazy). To complement my country man who is building me a log house in the woods, repairing everything that breaks down. Not to mention my Divine man. Nothing we cannot fix together. Even broken hearts are restored through our union.

Longingly, Pandora

☞ **In China, sandals without a heel strap are viewed as bedroom slippers and are generally considered inappropriate outdoor footwear.**

Dear Hermes,

I would always come out onto the balcony in the mornings in my worn leather sandals. I remember a man who stood on that balcony occasionally. He could tell the weather and make love; both he did with considerable skill and devotion, mostly unerringly. I did not love him, but he was worth keeping around. I liked to watch him standing naked on the back deck, smelling the air, a cup of coffee in his hand, turning slowly toward me and then coming indoors to report on the state of the sky. I tell you about him, Hermes, only because your skill is greater than his. And he had no demons, which made him impossible to love.

Love, Pandora

☞ **To cope with the vagaries of foreign bathrooms, consider wearing a long, full skirt. This will allow for some modesty in situations where you have to "go" outdoors. In parts of Asia or Africa, expect a jug of water, left beside the toilet, in lieu of paper. The smell in toilets is sometimes overpowering. Try dabbing some mentholatum under your nose to help mask the odours while you use the facilities.**

Wear expensive French perfume and think of the one you love, the one who gave it to you. Date all the brothers in the family, playing one off against the other, until you make your choice. Abandon deodorant. Let him follow your scent. Ask him to marry you. Let him think he is playing Cain, and wander the desert many centuries with him at your side. Follow his scent. Find the oasis, but let him think it was his map that got you there. Ignore the bad breath of camels at night, forced as you are to sleep close to them for their body heat. Recall the smell of his sweat rolling down his sides when you danced naked in the living room. Remember your lover's body beside yours on the first night you lived together, all your unpacked moving boxes around you where you lay on the mattress on the floor, only the stereo set up. No sheets, just the music and the ceiling. As soft as the stars above you now. And his smell as apparent to you as the exhalation of the stars: all that light inside him. Pull his old wool sweater around your shoulders and smell his lingering power.

My dear Hermes,

I have carried your sweater with me for several weeks, but cannot keep the chill of the mountain air from my bones. There is only your smell in the wool, but you are gone far from me. You gave me the gift of my voice, but what good does it do to wail about your absence in my life? How can I paint rainbows for you when I only have these blues?

                                        Still love you, Pandora

☞ **Keep all valuables in the elastic waistband of your knickers, or in a moneybelt tied around your waist. Wear a wide peasant skirt so that you can urinate quickly in open latrines without getting your clothes wet, and so that your moneybelt remains less visible.**

Wear expensive French panties underneath this wide skirt so that you can overcome the feeling of being a bag lady. Remember that, no matter how horrid a day you are having, if you are wearing nice knickers, life is good. Carry a photograph of the lingam of Shiva in your wallet. Tighten the moneybelt against your sweating hips and belly. Carry your cash in a separate belt from your ID and credit cards, so that if one is stolen, you will not be without resources. Curse your ancestors for being short-waisted and rounded as the bulk around your middle expands. Imagine that you are a kangaroo carrying her young in her pouch. Or imagine that you are already carrying the child of Hermes.

Dear Hermes,
I am wide, full, for you. My desire makes me want to look under every longhi, every kilt, to see whether or not there are men who are built like you. Just one reminder, please. In one city I visited, I slept on the floor along with all the other revellers, trying to sleep off the drugs. Earlier in the evening, I had wondered why my brilliant

friend should be enamoured of the stupid boy who was her fiancé. In the middle of the night, I watched him trip across the sleeping bodies, hauling his naked flesh toward the toilet, and suddenly I understood what she saw in him, saw it in the long silhouette he made in the bathroom light. How glorious! It was another of your manifestations, Hermes.

Just this morning, do spring out of bed for me, salute me "good morning." Imagine I would be there to lower your flagpole, patriot that I am. I miss you and I want to touch you over and over, my Joy-giver Hermes.

You reached under my skirt and you found my G spot! *Gracias a la vida!* Gravitas. Gravid. Gravity. How you ground me when I want to take flight, flee this world. I am your Aphrodite. I have no shame and will expose myself to you, stand on the half-shell, behind the fig leaf. In this entire global village where all the parts of the whole link up, I am getting closer to you, connected as we are through e-mails and cellphones and jets. We will stitch together a family with frequent flyer points, and our friendships with others will remain healthy with regular exercise of the fax and the answering machine. But, my darling Hermes, that one attachment that usually joins us together seems to be moving further and further apart, like the universe after the Big Bang! And time and the world are ever in flight! Where we were once creatures of the Earth (you slithering toward me in the middle of the night), we fly by air, always flitting about, stretched across oceans and continents, always "just arrived" or "just about to run," always conscious of other places and absences. I have seven phone numbers for you in my address book, but still cannot reach you. And how I desire to reach for you!

That act we perform over and over, with infinite variations on a theme once known, knowing it can never be known again in the same way, if at all. Still, I take heart. I know it's coming to me. You are coming to me. Everything is coming to me. Everything is coming alive. *Good night, sweet prince. And flights of angels sing thee to thy rest.*

Longingly,
Pandora

☞ **Use a compact, zippered bag with secret pockets. Don't carry anything you are afraid to lose.**

So you see, my dear, I was right not to take your heart along after all. Even though you are honoured among all the gods as a thief yourself, and stole my heart long ago.

Love,
Pandora

☞ **Outside North America, a one-piece swimsuit is always a safer choice than a bikini. Yet, in some countries, local women might swim entirely clothed, in accordance with their religious beliefs.**

And how many of those women really believe that the water will not swim between their thighs so lovingly that their faith will be restored? When they are conditioned by religion to be waiting, always waiting, for what comes after all their pain? What awaits them in the next life? What gratifying answers will await them if they hold out day and night, cooling their flushed cheeks against their cool clay houses the way their sisters across the ocean wait by the side of the telephone waiting for his voice? When that state of waiting leaves them longing, what better can they do than fling themselves fully clothed into the nearest stream and let their wet clothing rub their eager nipples? May there always be cool, clear, flowing water to drown the dissatisfaction of women who receive no gratification in the present!

Sweet Hermes,

Since you asked me the last time we spoke, I have thought long and hard about the answer to your question. What is it that women really want? I'll tell you, my love. Women want the perfect travelling hat. I have tried over and over again, paddled all over the world, but I have never found it. Leather is too heavy, too hot, and smells of oily scalp (perfectly acceptable on the gorgeous Argentinian gaucho when I rode behind him in the saddle, but hardly an odour I want for myself). And every straw hat I have owned has blown away or fallen apart.

Crocheted cotton droops unbecomingly after a while. Have you seen me in a baseball cap, honey? Forget it. Wide-brimmed wool hats never keep my ears warm enough, and the rain destroys them. Toques ruin my hairdo and I refuse to walk around all day with hat head. Bed head is something altogether different. Some days I am tempted to take a compass and draw a wide circle on canvas — a dunce's cap — maybe that would protect me from the elements! A Tilley is quite silly, no matter how endurable. Do you remember that shop in Portland, where we stood in front of the mirrors and tried on Tilleys? Then we ran back to our hotel room and laughed hysterically, composing our own survival stories: How we floated down the Amazon by inflating our Tilleys. How we used our Tilleys to skydive, hanging onto the string ties for dear life. How we hid our genitals from God with only a Tilley in front of our naked bodies. How you disguised yourself as a woman at the border, using both our Tilleys to stuff your shirt. Really, Hermes, you are such a ham! Adorable, if not more endurable than a Tilley.

But to get back to the perfect travelling hat. The point is, we want something that has a lifetime guarantee. That affords protection from all that falls upon our heads. AND we want style. We may change hats, but what we desire is constant.

Above all, my darling Hermes, remember this, and keep it under your hat: I am always watching over you, seeing you. You are never, never alone, even when you are indulging in your most outlandish pranks. Lately my eyes keep sweeping open skies, but not one song of heroic glory, not one other face or story, could ever win my heart away from you.

Yours throughout time,
Pandora

Acknowledgements

I wish to thank the following:

Carol Matthews, my constant reader and wise owl; Elizabeth McLean, my patient editor; Katharina Rout, my sister; Hiro Boga, my other sister; Ron Bonham, brilliant reader; Keith Harrison, fellow writer; Malaspina University-College; Thora Howell, our community support. And above all, Sheila Watson.

LIZA POTVIN was born in France and has lived in Canada for many years. Her stories and poems have appeared in numerous Canadian and American publications. Her book *White Lies* (NeWest) won the Edna Staebler Award for Creative Nonfiction in 1992. Liza teaches at Malaspina University College in Nanaimo, British Columbia.